A Million
SECONDS TOO LATE

Joygopal Podder

Vitasta
Let Knowledge Spread

Times Group Books

Published by Renu Kaul Verma for
Vitasta Publishing Pvt. Ltd.
2/15, Ansari Road, Daryaganj,
New Delhi - 110 002
info@vitastapublishing.com
ISBN 978-93-80828-74-9

This is a work of fiction. Certain descriptions of events have been inspired from real life incidents. The story, plot and incidents described, however, are all figments of the imagination of the author and the characters of this novel bear no resemblance to any person whatsoever, living or dead.

Cover Design and Layout by Vitasta Publishing Pvt. Ltd.

Printed by De Unique, New Delhi

Marketed and Distributed exclusively in India & Sub-Continent by:

Times Group Books

Times Group Books
(A division of Bennett, Coleman and Company Limited)
Times Annexe, Express Building
9-10 Bahadur Shah Zafar Marg, New Delhi-110 002

"Dedicated to my Parents, Wife and my Daughters."

Of all sad words of tongue or pen,
the saddest are these: "It might have been!"

– John Greenleaf Whittier

Contents

1
Tragedy

Sujata Malhotra woke up suddenly with a deep sense of alarm. Something had disturbed her sleep. A loud noise – the sound of breaking glass.

She sat up in bed, holding her nightgown tightly against her body. Instinctively, her hand groped the left side of the bed. Then her hand stopped moving. The left side of the bed was empty. Her husband was not lying next to her.

Then Sujata remembered. Devesh was not at home tonight. He wasn't even in town.

The recollection brought with it a deeper sense of dread. She would have to face some unknown danger alone...

In the predawn hush around her, Sujata heard nothing. Had she been mistaken? Was the sound that she felt she had heard, a part of a broken dream – of which she now had no memory?

Sujata held her breath. The house was still and quiet. The deep silence around her continued unbroken. The dull red night lamp, in a corner of the bedroom, glowed faintly and reassuringly – go back to sleep, it seemed to urge. Sujata's racing pulse began to slow down. Her heartbeats gradually retraced from frantic pumping to a more sedate and familiar rhythm.

Sujata Malhotra relaxed. She had been disturbed by a bad dream. She slowly leaned backwards and placed her head back on her pillow. She closed her eyes.

Her simple decision to go back to sleep would haunt Sujata Malhotra and keep her in deep grief for the rest of her life…

How long Sujata Malhotra slept she could not later recall. What she did remember clearly was that she was again woken up quite suddenly by a loud noise. This time it was not a sound of breaking glass. And this time, there was no doubt in her mind, that it was a real – not imagined – noise.

Sujata had been woken up by a strangled cry…

Sujata Malhotra sat up in her bed, wondering what she should do now. She hurriedly felt for the switch of the reading lamp, on the side table next to the bed and pressed it down. The light bulb switched on and bathed Sujata in its comforting yellow glow. She groped for the handle of the drawer of the side table and pulled out a torch. Feeling more confident now, Sujata swung her feet off the bed and, putting on her slippers, stood up, the nightgown held tightly around her. The hum of the airconditioner in her bedroom could not drown out the next sound that hit Sujata's ears – a baleful moan.

Sujata Malhotra's blood froze. What kind of a sound was this?

Panic gripped Sujata. Was the sound of breaking glass that had earlier disturbed her sleep, caused by a toppling glass of water in one of the rooms of the children? Had a half-asleep child stepped on broken glass?

Sujata sprang to action. She would need to investigate the cause of these disturbing sounds immediately. She quickly navigated to the door of the master bedroom which she shared with her husband and stepped out into the corridor.

There it was again – the strange baleful moaning sound. Where was it coming from?

The door of the master bedroom opened into a corridor that led to four other bedrooms. The children slept in these four bedrooms. The bedroom on Sujata's right was occupied by her stepson Rajat. Her stepson, like her husband, was not in town. The sound of moaning had also not emerged from Rajat's room, which was anyway empty. This narrowed down the search a little.

The sound had also not come from the room across from the master bedroom, which was occupied by the youngest children, her own children – Renu and Nikhil. Sujata turned her eyes in the direction of the two doors, side by side, at the end of the corridor.

The disturbance was in one of the bedrooms occupied by the twenty four year old twin sisters Aradhana and Anamika, her step daughters.

There it was again – the moaning sound, softer now. Much softer. Sujata's pulse quickened. One of the elder girls was in some kind of trouble. Forgetting to switch on the lights of the corridor in her hurry, Sujata turned on the torch and quickly marched towards Aradhana's room. She paused outside the door. There was no sound coming from inside the room.

Sujata stepped over to the next door – the one at the extreme end of the corridor that housed all the five bedrooms. She felt she heard a movement from inside the room – and did not hesitate a moment longer. Sujata turned the door handle. The door was not locked from inside. She swung the door open and stepped inside, the light from her torch spraying the room with its bright yellow glow.

Then Sujata Malhotra screamed out in horror…

There was a masked figure standing at the head of Anamika's bed. The figure looked to be that of a man – a tall man in dark clothes. He had been half bent down when Sujata had walked into the room. There was a knife in his hand. The knife was dripping blood.

Sujata continued screaming as the torchlight exposed the nightmarish scene on the bed. The girl, Anamika, was drenched in blood from her head to the middle of her body.

The masked man swung around and stared at Sujata Malhotra as she turned and fled the room, screaming all the while in a demented frenzy of horror and fear…

***

2

Broken Window and Bloodied Bed

"The poor girl stood no chance," commented Rajeev Srivastava sadly. "Anamika was dead when her mother discovered her."

Detective Superintendent Avinash Sharma of the Gurgaon Police Crime Branch said nothing. He simply stared down at the bloodied body of the dead girl lying on the blood drenched bed. His face was expressionless – masking his emotions which were anything but peaceful at this moment.

The autopsy report would later state clinically what Avinash Sharma could make out already – the girl Anamika Malhotra had been bludgeoned repeatedly on the head with a hammer or a similar instrument with a conical or triangular head. She had also been stabbed as many as eight times in the neck, chest and abdomen.

Her hands, knees and right foot bore signs of defensive wounds. Anamika had died fighting.

"The killer escaped by the same route through which he had entered," observed Detective Inspector Ramesh Uppal, an earnest looking police officer aged thirty five years, and Avinash's lieutenant for the last two years, as he adjusted his spectacles and looked grimly at the broken window.

The shattered glass of the window, the breaking of which had woken up Sujata Malhotra the first time during that nightmarish night, lay strewn on the floor of the dead girl's bedroom, just below the opening which had apparently facilitated the entry and exit of the killer.

The broken window and the bloodied bed were the only disturbing elements in the room. Everything else was perfectly in place – the furniture, the display items, the photographs and pictures on the walls. The cupboard doors had not been forced open. The drawers had not been ransacked.

Either the killer had not had the time to steal anything before he had been disturbed by Sujata – or he had not entered the bedroom to rob but had come simply to kill.

The question that begged an answer, of course, was – why would anybody want to murder Anamika Malhotra?

As the forensic experts went about their jobs all around him, picking up fingerprints from furniture and fixtures and organizing photographs of the dead girl from different angles, Detective Superintendent Avinash Sharma looked around the room, one last time, in a vain hope for some clue to the riddle. There was, of course, no such clue to be seen. In fact, jewellery and a wallet lying on the dead girl's dressing table had apparently not been disturbed – making a stronger case for the belief that the killer had not been a robber who had been disturbed in the act of stealing but was someone who had made an entry into the bedroom with the specific purpose of committing murder….

Detective Superintendent Avinash Sharma turned and left the bedroom of the dead girl, vowing silently to himself that he would track down her killer, come what may.

***

3

A Night of Horror

Avinash Sharma would have to wait for a better opportunity and time to meet the mistress of the house. But he already knew the details of the horror she had gone through only a few hours before. Rajeev Srivastava, who lived next door, had already told him.

Sujata Malhotra was closeted in her room, deeply sedated. The lady had shown tremendous presence of mind in the middle of the night, immediately before the predawn hours – but now the shock and reaction had set in.

Displaying an admirable presence of mind in the middle of such horrifying circumstances, Sujata Malhotra had remembered, while rushing out of Anamika's room, to press the button located on the wall between the doors that separated the two bedrooms of her step-daughters that activated a siren-style burglar alarm outside the house. She had then banged on the Aradhana's door, screaming all the while, before remembering to check whether it was unlocked.

The bedroom door was unlocked – so she rushed in. A deeply startled and white faced Aradhana was already awake and half out of her bed when Sujata had rushed in. "What – what – what", she had exclaimed, all remnants of sleep disappearing when she had seen the face of her devastated step-mother.

Sujata had simply grabbed Aradhana's hand and rushed out of the room – straight into Anamika's bedroom, displaying admirable courage. But it had been too late.

The killer had disappeared, apparently through the same window from which he had made his entrance. As Aradhana began screaming at the terrible sight of her brutalized and bloodied sister lying on the bed, Sujata felt for Anamika's pulse.

There was no pulse.

Two security guards who were stationed at the gate of the mansion had run up to the main door of the house at the sound of the burglar alarm that Sujata had activated. A startled and frightened servant had let them in – and the guards had rushed up to the first floor where the rooms were located.

One sight of the bloodied body on the bed had activated the guards into a frenzy of action. One had screamed into his walkie-talkie to his other two colleagues at the gate, who immediately began scouring the grounds of the mansion for the escaping killer. The guards inside the house had then quickly joined their colleagues outside, but to no avail.

The only tell-tale sign of breaking-and-entering that the security guards found was a long rope hanging from the side of the wall, in one corner of the rear of the small estate. The killer had evidently made his entry by climbing over the wall in that remote corner of the compound.

Next door, Rajeev Srivastava, and his wife, Renuka, were awakened by the shrill burglar alarm. Mrs Srivastava immediately ran out into the backyard of her own house to look for intruders but saw nothing.

Moments later, the couple's phone rang; it was a servant from the Malhotra household, urgently asking for the doctor to come and help Anamika. Rajeev Srivastava had quickly pulled on trousers over his pajamas and hurried over to the Malhotra mansion and then up the flight of stairs to Anamika's room.

It was no use. Anamika was long gone.

Rajeev Srivastava had then picked up the nearest telephone and called the police emergency number....

***

4

Deep Grief

When Detective Superintendent Avinash Sharma returned to the main drawing room of the Malhotra mansion, which was located on the ground floor of the palatial house, after his brief and somber inspection of the first floor bedroom of the unfortunate girl, he was met by her twin sister.

Sitting on each side of Aradhana Malhotra were her younger stepsister and stepbrother, the children of Sujata Malhotra, Renu and Nikhil. The girl was just under ten years of age, Avinash Sharma knew, and the boy was only eight years old. They looked remarkably composed for two small children, who had been witness to such a terrible tragedy, in their own house, just a few hours before.

Aradhana Malhotra also looked composed. Her eyes were very red; she had evidently been crying. However, she was clearly trying to keep her emotions in control for the sake of the children. Her stoic composure, in the face of such a horrible experience of seeing the bludgeoned and stabbed body of her twin sister, was praiseworthy. Avinash Sharma was moved and impressed.

He sat down on a nearby sofa but said nothing.

Aradhana spoke. Her voice was controlled. "What now?"

Avinash looked at the children before answering and tried to keep his reply as brief and unemotional as possible. "Your sister will be taken to the hospital. The forensic experts are checking the room for any clues left behind by the intruder."

Aradhana beckoned to a maid who was standing nearby. She gripped the shoulders of her younger siblings and said softly: "Why don't you both go to the family lounge and watch some television? Neha will make you some snacks to eat. I will join you shortly...."

Renu and Nikhil got up obediently. They followed the maid out of the room.

Aradhana Malhotra turned to face the Detective Superintendent. Her eyes were blazing. "You'd better find the killer fast!" she said, her voice choking. "My sister's death must be avenged!"

Avinash Sharma was slightly taken aback. "We will do our best," he replied grimly. "We will leave no stone unturned to track down the murderer of your sister."

Aradhana was quiet for a while. Then she said: "Dad is on a plane heading back to Delhi right now. He was in Jaipur last night."

'Dad' was Devesh Malhotra, the famous industrialist and shipping magnate, who had very recently been appointed a member of the Economic Advisory Council that was chaired by none other than the Prime Minister of India. Devesh Malhotra was one of the most well connected and influential people in the country. Detective Superintendent Avinash Sharma was well aware of the tremendous political pressure that would be put on his superiors and on him to expeditiously solve this murder.

"And your brother?"

Aradhana Malhotra grimaced. "I'm unable to connect with him. His cellphone is switched off. I've sent him an SMS. When he reads it, I'm sure he will call back immediately."

Avinash Sharma was surprised. "You mean that you don't know where your brother is right now?" he asked, trying not to show his amazement. A shadow passed over the attractive face of Aradhana Malhotra. She kept quiet.

Detective Superintendent Avinash studied the young lady in front of him. He had already studied the features of the dead sister – and it was obvious that there had been a strong resemblance between the siblings, who had been born on the same day around the same time. Avinash did not know who had entered the world first, but that piece of information would be a mere technicality, he was sure. The twin sisters had almost – though not exactly – identical features.

Aradhana was extremely good looking. The forty year old Avinash was about sixteen years older to the young lady in front of him, and the circumstances of their meeting were extremely unfortunate, but that did not prevent him from appreciating the fact that he was sitting opposite a raven-haired beauty. Aradhana also looked extremely strong willed – as probably befitted the daughter of a tycoon.

She now spoke: "My sister was extremely disturbed during the last few days. This could have a bearing on her murder – though I can't, of course be sure. But you must check this aspect out, Superintendent!"

Avinash Sharma stiffened. This could prove to be an important lead. He said seriously: "Please tell me whatever is on your mind – don't hold anything back. Let me decide whether your information has a bearing on your sister's death or not. I must investigate all possibilities, no matter how remote the apparent connection!"

Aradhana was quiet again. She looked contemplative. There was also another expression on her face. Was it anxiety, Avinash wondered, or was it something closer to fear?

Aradhana began speaking again: "Anamika and I did not get to meet up much in the last few months, although we did stay under the same roof. I had joined one of my father's companies, where I am still working. Anamika had joined a childcare organization that runs orphanages. We both had very separate professional and personal lives. But, a few nights ago, she met me just before dinner and spoke to me for the first time of death threats…."

Detective Superintendent Avinash Sharma's blood froze. "Death threats against Anamika?" he asked with foreboding.

When Aradhana replied, her voice was shaking: "No, against me…"

***

5

The Brother

Around the same time that the unfortunate girl Anamika was being bludgeoned and stabbed to death in New Delhi's posh suburb Gurgaon, the night guard Mohan Bhisht was patrolling the cargo terminal at Mumbai's Chattrapati Shivaji International Airport, located in the area known as Sahar.

In the predawn hours, Mohan Bhisht spotted a black Maruti Eeco van pulling into a bay near a loading platform, that was used to send parcels and boxes for storage, in the high security vaults of the cargo terminal.

Puzzled, Mohan Bhisht began walking towards the loading bay to investigate this peculiar apparition. As far as he knew, no loading or unloading activity was scheduled at this hour of the night.

As he approached the black van, Mohan suddenly felt something very hard strike his head with great force.

He crumpled to the ground with blinding pain as blood began to pour from the wound that had been caused to his head by the crushing blow.

A slim man wearing a black mask over his face, with only his eyes and lips exposed, stepped out of the darkness and pointed the .45 pistol, the barrel of which had been used to strike down the night guard, directly at Mohan's head.

"Don't utter a sound!" snarled the slim man in the black mask, whose name was Rajat Malhotra and who was the son of the tycoon Devesh Malhotra.

Another masked man appeared and grabbed the guard's gun. The night guard was disarmed.

"Get up!" hissed Rajat Malhotra.

As the bleeding night guard struggled to his feet, Rajat pointed his pistol at a box fixed to a nearby wall.

"Disconnect the alarm!" Rajat ordered him.

Still in pain – and wondering how these strange and dangerous masked men knew of the location of the alarm box – he did as he was ordered.

After he had disconnected the alarm, the still bleeding night guard's hands were handcuffed behind his back.

Another night guard, Jagat Singh, had heard the noise caused by the falling body of Mohan Bhisht. He came over to the loading ramp to investigate – and was immediately surrounded by three armed and masked men who promptly disarmed and handcuffed him.

The guard Jagat Singh carried the only key that allowed entry into the cargo terminal building through a side door. The masked men appeared to know this. Rough hands felt his trouser and jacket pockets and quickly discovered the precious key.

The five masked and armed gunmen and their two prisoners then entered the cargo terminal building.

One of the largest cash robberies to be ever committed on Indian soil was about to take place....

***

6

The Twin Sister

Detective Inspector Ramesh Uppal joined Avinash Sharma and Aradhana Malhotra. He kept standing, in deference to his senior, and cast an appreciative eye over Aradhana's face. Then he noticed the serious look on her face, which was reflected also on the face of his superior, and Ramesh Uppal's mind leapfrogged to attention.

Detective Superintendent Avinash Sharma spoke with great urgency. "What death threats have you been getting?" he asked Aradhana quickly. "And how did Anamika get to know of them?"

Aradhana's eyes welled up. She did not reply directly to Avinash's queries. Instead, she focused on another thought. "If Anamika has been murdered because her killer thought he was attacking me, I will never be able to live with this guilt!"

Avinash and Ramesh remained silent, their minds ablaze with

conjecture and queries.

Aradhana continued: "Anamika told me that there were two death threats. They were received by Anamika but, in one, she was addressed as Aradhana!"

The two officers stared at each other. Their minds carried the same thought. The chances that Anamika had been killed by a burglar caught in a random act of theft were now beginning to look remote. If Aradhana was speaking the truth – and there appeared to be no reason why she would not be – this killing had a deeper story behind it....

Detective Superintendent Avinash Sharma decided to waste no more time in getting to the facts. "Can you tell me the whole story, please?" he asked politely but firmly.

Aradhana composed herself. "Of course!" she responded contritely. "I'm sorry I'm speaking in riddles. This is not helping you at all! Here are the full details..."

"Anamika got the first threat over a landline phone at her office around two weeks ago," said Aradhana. "She told me that the voice was that of a man. She did not recognize it. It was an unfamiliar voice. The man told her to mind her own business – or else she would not live for very long. The phone was disconnected immediately after that. It was a very direct threat and it unnerved my sister – though she eventually convinced herself that it was a nasty prank."

"The telephone instrument had no caller identification

facility?" asked Ramesh Uppal.

"No, though it was installed after Anamika complained to her superior that she was getting prank calls," replied Aradhana.

"What made Anamika think that the threat was against you and not her?" asked Avinash Sharma.

"Because the caller addressed her twice as Aradhana while making his threat...."

Avinash Sharma and Ramesh Uppal digested this piece of information very thoughtfully.

Avinash then asked carefully: "Have you been involved in any activity that could have resulted in such a threat against you?"

Aradhana Malhotra's response shocked the two police officers. "I can't answer that question right now," she replied.

***

7

The Heist

Inside the cargo terminal building, the five masked and armed gunmen and their two prisoners found themselves in the middle of a maze of corridors. The gunmen were unfazed. They had either carefully studied the plans of the building beforehand or had received inside help and information from one or more of the staff working in these premises.

It was actually a combination of both factors that gave the robbers the confidence to navigate through the corridors and march their captives straight to the cafeteria where five other cargo terminal employees were partaking of refreshments during their 4 am break.

The five masked gunmen burst into the cafeteria, brandishing their firearms and pushing their prisoners before them. The five employees of the cargo terminal, who were inside the room, all jumped to their feet with shock, their meals forgotten.

"Stay completely still!" commanded Rajat Malhotra. "Whoever makes even the slightest of moves will end up like your friend here!" Rajat pointed his gun at the bleeding head of Mohan Bhisht.

The threat worked – the five men stood completely still. Only their eyes moved – registering shock, fear and a little anger.

The handcuffed Mohan Bhisht and Jagat Singh, the night guards who had been on duty outside the building only a little while before, were pushed to the ground and made to lie face down. "Lie very still and you will not be harmed," Rajat told them, while his fellow gunmen busied themselves handcuffing the five cargo terminal staff. Then four of the five men were also pushed to the ground and made to lie face down.

Only Prasad Dhingra, the terminal's senior cargo agent, was allowed to remain standing.

Rajat Malhotra was clearly the leader of the group of robbers – he was doing all the talking. He turned his masked face in the direction of Prasad Dhingra and said: "You are the senior cargo agent, aren't you?"

Prasad Dhingra was too frightened to ask back how the gunman holding the .45 pistol knew this. He simply nodded his head in assent.

Rajat pointed his gun in the direction of the intercom. "Pick up that phone," he commanded, "and speak to Krishna Lele!"

Krishna Lele was another night guard – the only guard on

duty that night who knew the right combinations to open the double door vault, located in the lower basement of the cargo terminal. The employees, held captive by the gunmen, could clearly make out that the robbers were very well informed and had come to this mission of theirs armed, not just with guns and daring – but with a lot of inside knowledge and details.

As the frightened and shaking Prasad walked over to the intercom instrument and picked up the receiver, Rajat continued with his instructions: "Tell Krishna that there appears to be a problem with a consignment that came in from Bangkok yesterday. Tell him that you've just received information that there could be a security issue with one of the cartons."

As Prasad began pushing the intercom buttons to make his call, as per the instructions, this leader of the gunmen pronounced one more dire warning: "Don't try to pass on any warning signal to Krishna. We know everything about you and your families," Rajat's eyes swept over not just Prasad Dhingra but all the other cargo terminal staff and guards lying face down on the ground, "and we have men stationed outside each one of your residences waiting to pay a visit to your families in case you try anything funny here! So be very careful...."

***

8

Secrets

A young woman had been cruelly murdered, while she had been sleeping in her own bedroom, not very many hours ago. The murdered girl's step-mother had probably seen her dying and also glimpsed her murderer – and now the elder woman was lying in a state of shock and sedated. Against the background of these circumstances, Detective Superintendent Avinash Sharma of the Gurgaon police was in no mood to take any nonsense from the twin sister of the murdered girl. If Aradhana had knowledge that could lead to the capture of Anamika's murderer – she would have to come clean with it whether she liked it or not…

"I don't understand, Miss Malhotra," said Avinash Sharma, with barely suppressed anger, "If you have been involved in any activity that could have resulted in a threat being made against you, then clearly it is an important matter, which needs to be shared with the team investigating your sister's murder. She received a threat in your name. She may have been killed instead of you, by mistake! How can you suppress information that could probably lead us to the killer?"

Aradhana Malhotra's face flushed. "I'm not a fool, Superintendent!" she retorted. "I understand all the implications. I also understand that, if I was the real target, then I am still in very great danger…"

"Then why are you not telling us why there should be a threat to your life?" "Because the reasons that make me think so are not conclusive – I need to find out a few more things before I can decide that I am not letting my imagination run wild…"

Avinash almost had a fit. "Shouldn't you let the investigating agencies decide this?" he retorted, this time not bothering to hide his anger. "Your sister has just been brutally murdered – and you're playing games with the police?"

Aradhana bit her lips to hold back her own anger at being spoken to so roughly. "I am not playing games, Superintendent!" she threw back. "You asked me a very clear question: am I involved in any activity that could have resulted in a death threat against me? My answer is also clear and straightforward: I don't know!" She stared straight and hard at Avinash Sharma. "You have also not heard the complete story regarding the threats. The second death threat was directed specifically against Anamika herself – it was her name which was printed on the envelope, which carried the note in which was the second threat!"

***

9

The Treasure in the Vault

Prasad Dhingra's phone call was effective – a very alarmed Krishna Lele rushed to the cafeteria, to learn more about the perceived security threat in the previous day's consignment from Bangkok.

The night guard was caught completely by surprise when, on entering the cafeteria, he was met by two shotguns pointed at his head.

The sight of the cargo terminal staff lying handcuffed and face down on the ground made him realize the full implications of what was going on. He was promptly disarmed by one of the gunmen.

Rajat and two other masked gunmen took custody of Krishna Lele. "Take us to the vault!" Rajat ordered the stunned night guard, as he pushed him out of the cafeteria at gunpoint.

The remaining two robbers continued guarding the five immobilized cargo terminal staff, including the hapless senior cargo agent Prasad Dhingra, who had also been forced to the ground and handcuffed, his task over.

Later, Krishna would report to the police that the three masked and armed gunmen, who forced him to lead them to the cargo terminal vault, already knew its location – and everything else about it. The robbers confidently took him, at gun point, down two flights of stairs to the double door vault. He later reported that the gunmen knew all about the safety systems in the vault and also about the double door system, whereby one door needed to be shut before the other one was opened, or otherwise, the alarm at the central security office in the main airport terminal building would be activated.

As they stood before the entrance to the vault, Rajat motioned to Krishna with his gun to open the twelve inches thick metal door.

Krishna could make out that any resistance would be futile and foolhardy. He pressed the right numbers on the panel at the centre of the door. The correct combination activated the locking system – there was a loud click, and then one of the gunmen pulled at the door handle. The iron door swung open.

The three gunmen and their prisoner stepped into a ten-by-twenty foot room. "Shut the door!" ordered Rajat harshly.

Krishna complied.

"Now, open the second door".

Krishna did the needful – since the first door had been shut, the opening of the second door would not activate the alarm. He marveled at the prior knowledge and preparedness of the robbers.

The second door of the cargo terminal vault swung open. The robbers and the night guard stepped inside.

"Lie on the ground – face down!" Rajat Malhotra ordered Krishna. The night guard did as he was told - and was immediately handcuffed with his hands tied behind his back.

The robbers then got to work. They had a specific target in mind – Rajat began sifting through the invoices and freight manifests lying on a table near the vault entrance, to determine which parcels they wanted, out of the many similarly wrapped ones stacked inside the room.

The target of the robbers was a consignment from Kathmandu. The parcels contained cash – untraceable money to the tune of about three million dollars, taken from collections at several casinos run by the Indian mafia in the capital city of Nepal.

The consignment from Kathmandu was quickly identified. Twenty parcels were removed from the storage racks and placed by the three gunmen in the ten-by-twenty foot room immediately outside the vault.

Their job over, the robbers turned their attention back to Krishna. One of Rajat's colleagues pulled up the night guard from the ground and the other gunman removed his handcuffs.

The four men stepped out of the vault into the room where the parcels were already stacked. "Lock the inner door before unlocking the outer door!" Rajat sternly reminded Krishna, in case he was harboring any thoughts of a last minute activation of the alarm by opening both vault doors together.

Krishna knew better than to invite certain death by trying to act smart. He repeated the earlier process of locking one door before unlocking the second.

After the outer door was also locked, the night guard was escorted back to the cafeteria by Rajat while the other two gunmen began the laborious task of carrying the parcels, in instalments, to the door on the ground floor that led outside and to their black van.

Back in the cafeteria, Krishna joined his colleagues on the floor, having been duly handcuffed.

As the three gunmen prepared to leave the cafeteria to join their colleagues in making their getaway, Rajat issued his parting shot to the helpless employees who were lying face down and handcuffed on the floor: "Do not attempt to make any move from the floor for at least thirty minutes," he ordered. "If you raise an alarm and the police catch us, our men will visit your residences and kill your families!" Rajat looked at the back of the head of the night guard Mohan Bhisht. The wound had dried up and there was a cake of matted blood around the gash, where the barrel of the pistol had struck. "Make sure to treat the wound first, before you do anything else," he advised while exiting the room, " and get a tetanus shot fast...."

The five gunmen made an easy getaway in their black Maruti Eeco van, carrying away the twenty parcels of cash that had arrived at the cargo terminal of Mumbai's Chattrapati Shivaji International Airport from Kathmandu, three days before.

The heist had taken just about sixty minutes and was one of the largest cash robberies to be ever committed on Indian soil. But for Rajat Malhotra, the leader of the gang, the predawn robbery had an even greater importance than the cash component – hidden inside one of the parcels was a list of candidates that the Indian mafia had finalized in a recent conclave in Kathmandu. These would be financed and helped to win, in the forthcoming by-elections to the Indian Parliament…

***

10

The Second Death Threat

"The second death threat was received by Anamika only a few days ago," Aradhana informed Detective Superintendent Avinash Sharma and Detective Inspector Ramesh Uppal. "It was that very evening that she met me and told me of the two death threats – one in my name and one, apparently, in her name."

"Why did you say 'apparently'"? asked Ramesh Uppal puzzled.

"Because the envelope which contained the threat carried Anamika's name but the note inside did not have any name mentioned on it. Against the background of the earlier threat, where the voice on the phone mentioned my name twice, there is room for some confusion," responded Aradhana.

"I agree," observed Avinash Sharma thoughtfully.

Aradhana continued: "The envelope was received by Anamika in her office. It came through the post. It carried her name and office address – as I've told you earlier, she used to work for a charitable childcare organization that runs several orphanages. The name and address had been printed from a computer, cut out from the printout and pasted on the envelope. There was no addressee mentioned on either side of the envelope. All this Anamika studied after reading the threat inside."

"The threat was also in the form of a computer printout," guessed Ramesh Uppal.

"Yes. There was only one line in the page. It read: 'Mind your own business or you'll die soon.' Anamika was very frightened – but, again, in the light of the earlier threat, she could not make out whether the threat was against her or me."

"Anamika kept quiet about the first threat but took both seriously after receiving the second one?" asked Avinash.

"Yes," replied Aradhana. "The earlier phone call she took to be a prank. Only after receiving the note through the post did she get all serious about the threats and confide in me."

"Did you then inform your parents, or brother or anybody else?" asked Avinash.

"No." Aradhana's voice choked with emotion. "I now dearly wish we had – perhaps this tragedy could have been averted!"

"Why did you keep quiet?" he asked.

Aradhana was silent for a moment. Then she spoke somberly. "It sounds a bit strange when put like this but both Anamika and I had quietly begun investigating some strange happenings in the separate organizations we were working for. This we confided to each other when my sister informed me of the death threats…"

Avinash Sharma and Ramesh Uppal stared at each other in amazement and then looked with heightened interest at Aradhana. "You mean both you and your sister had stumbled on suspicious activities at your respective places of work?" asked Avinash.

"Yes, Superintendent," responded Aradhana. "So we were confused as to who the death threats were directed at. It was clear that one of us at least was genuinely on the trail of suspicious activity; hence the death threats. We decided to delve a bit deeper before informing our parents and the police about the threats."

Avinash Sharma now understood. He held Aradhana's gaze and said: "You thought that there was some suspicious activity going on, in one of the companies belonging to your father which you had joined – and you wanted to check out whether your father, himself, was involved or not, isn't it?"

Aradhana Malhotra dropped her head and stared at her hands.

***

11

The Father

This was the moment that Devesh Malhotra arrived at his house and confronted the terrible tragedy that had befallen his family.

Devesh Malhotra was an imposing man. He was not very big in terms of physical size – his height was not more than five feet and eight inches or so – but he more than made up for the lack in height with the sheer magnetism of his personality.

The tycoon was no longer the dashing and sprightly young man with the playboy image that he had acquired in his thirties. He was now a powerful maker and breaker of destinies and a shaper of major events. And he looked the part.

Devesh Malhotra's thick head of hair was still black at the top but steel grey at the temples and he maintained short white sideburns. The effect was distinguished. His face was rugged and handsome – and the lines brought about by fifty-five years of hard and exciting living, only added to the appeal of his dynamic looks, that attracted women of substance to Devesh Malhotra like bees to honey.

Also adding to his dynamism was Devesh Malhotra's in-your-face arrogance. The world, according to this self-made tycoon, was made up of only two kinds of people: the achievers and the losers. The latter, Devesh Malhotra very well knew, formed the vast majority of the world's population. Devesh Malhotra also knew very well that he belonged firmly to the small group that formed the former category – and that he with his rags-to-riches story was a cut above even those who had reached positions of wealth and power, but had done so on the backs of families and legacies.

In short, Devesh Malhotra had made it on his own terms without giving a damn for what anybody thought of him and his methods – and he had no qualms in continuing to show his disdain, for those who he felt did not measure up to his high standards of intelligence, dynamism, and drive to succeed. In short, ninety five per cent of the world's population was not worth the time of the day for Devesh Malhotra.

This morning, however, he was a much mellowed man.

Aradhana Malhotra jumped to her feet at the sight of her father striding into the main drawing room of the palatial house. She ran to him and flung herself into his arms. Her loud sobs rent the air.

Detective Superintendent Avinash Sharma and Detective

Inspector Ramesh Uppal stood in uncomfortable silence as the father and daughter bonded together in deep grief.

Devesh Malhotra held his arms around his devastated daughter in a tight embrace. His face was composed but the pain in his eyes was undisguised.

In spite of himself, Detective Superintendent Avinash Sharma's eyes made their observations and his experienced mind arrived at its tentative conclusion: Here was a father who was completely shattered by his daughter's brutal murder. He may or may not have been a party to the alleged suspicious activities in his organisation – but he was not a party to his daughter's death...

Eventually, the father loosened his embrace and raised his daughter's face with his hands and looked deep into her eyes. "Remember Anamika as she was in her life, not as she was in her death, my baby," he said slowly to Aradhana, his eyes moist. Then Devesh Malhotra looked in the direction of the police officers and said in a voice of steel: "Whoever did this must pay, you understand?"

Avinash Sharma and Ramesh Uppal said nothing. They had heard almost the same sentiments uttered by the daughter not too long ago...

Devesh Malhotra looked at his daughter again. "Where is Anamika's body?" he asked.

Rajeev Srivastava entered the room at this moment. He answered the question. "Anamika's body has been taken in an ambulance to Vedanta Hospital."

Devesh Malhotra looked at the police officers again. "I would like to see my daughter for one last time," he said. It was a request but sounded more like a command.

Detective Superintendent Avinash simply nodded his head in assent. This was the least he could do for the distraught father.

"Where's your mother?" Devesh asked Aradhana. She told him.

"The poor poor woman!" he exclaimed. "God only knows what a terrible experience she has been through! Let's go to her…"

As the father and daughter moved towards the stairs leading to the first floor bedrooms, Aradhana's cellphone beeped. The young lady peered at the number on the screen. She immediately punched the 'answer' button and exclaimed into the phone: "Bhai, where are you? Something terrible has happened…"

The family was now together in its grief.

***

12

The Doctor

As the father and daughter duo went to meet the sedated and resting mother in the master bedroom of the palatial house, Avinash Sharma, accompanied by Ramesh Uppal and the Malhotra's neighbor Rajeev Srivastava, went outside the building to inspect what his men had discovered after scouring the lawns and gardens of the mansion.

The various items that the police teams had discovered on the grounds of the property were varied and of indeterminate relevance to the murder investigation. There was a rusty knife, a broken bottle, a slipper, a one hundred rupee note, a yellow colored plastic wristband with the words "A Second Chance" written in red letters, a pack of playing cards, an inexpensive gent's wristwatch in surprisingly good condition, a cigarette lighter, a plastic tiffin box and a hair brush.

Detective Inspector Ramesh Uppal scratched his head and pushed his spectacles back over the bridge of his nose. "This is all regular junk," he observed. "The gardens of this house must be used often, I suppose, by the children and their friends for playing, and by the adults for hosting parties – hence the accumulation of all this clutter on the lawns and in the bushes."

"I guess you're right," commented Avinash Sharma. "Nevertheless, we must send everything we gather at or near the crime scene to the laboratory for testing – you never know what unexpected findings might turn up!"

"Of course!" agreed Ramesh Uppal. He turned to another police officer and asked: "Anything special or interesting discovered from the dead girl's room?"

The answer was in the negative. Nothing incriminating had been left behind in the murdered girl's room by the killer. There was no trace of a potential weapon – there was no clue to the perpetrator of the crime.

"We will have to go into the life stories of the dead girl and her family members to look for potential motives and suspects," observed Avinash Sharma. He turned to Rajeev Srivastava and asked: "What do you know about the dead girl Anamika?"

"I only know her as a neighbour," responded Srivastava. "Our families are not very close – Devesh Malhotra literally occupies another planet from the one I live on. He is extremely high profile and rich. I am fortunate to have some wealth of my own – and a flourishing medical practice – but I am way out of Devesh's league. Hence, my interaction with his family has been limited to only some social get togethers and purely professional interaction."

"Professional interaction? Do you mean you are the family doctor?"

"No, not that. I run a state-of the-art medical centre in the neighbourhood which the Malhotra family members visit occasionally for routine check-ups and during small health emergencies."

Avinash Sharma looked interested. "So you have an idea of Anamika Malhotra's medical history?" he asked.

Srivastava suddenly looked evasive. "I am aware of her health records, yes," he replied slowly.

Detective Superintendent Avinash and Detective Inspector Ramesh exchanged quick glances. The experienced pair had realised that this was a conversation that needed to be taken forward…

***

13

Medical History

Avinash Sharma and Ramesh Uppal were sitting on the first floor verandah of Srivastava's house, drinking cups of hot tea that had been served to them by Mrs Renuka Srivastava and snacking on lightly toasted egg sandwiches.

The dim light of the early morning had given way to delightful sunlight. It was going to be a beautiful autumn day. The greenery, for which the Delhi suburb of Gurgaon was justly famous, sparkled crisply in the reflected sunlight. It was difficult to believe that, only a few hours ago, in a horrible predawn nightmare, a young woman's life had been very brutally snuffed out by an unknown killer in the mansion next door.

Srivastava had temporarily avoided further questioning, on the health records of the dead girl, by inviting the two detectives to his house for tea and snacks. The police officers, who had been unceremoniously pulled out of their beds and homes in the very early hours by the emergency calls from the Malhotra mansion, were hungry and thirsty. Srivastava's invitation had been very welcome.

But now the questioning would have to resume. Srivastava, also sipping tea with his guests, was ready for the inevitable.

Detective Superintendent Avinash Sharma asked the question bluntly: "Did Anamika Malhotra visit your clinic recently with any medical problem, doctor?"

The doctor had been expecting the question, but he still looked a bit uncomfortable. "You are aware of course Superintendent, that there are certain matters which can only be discussed between doctor and patient – and cannot be shared with a third party?" he said as a way of response.

Avinash put down his cup and saucer with some force on the garden table in front of him. "What patient are you talking about, doctor?" he asked a bit harshly. "Are you referring to the girl who has just been beaten and stabbed to death in her bed? You want to keep to yourself information which could perhaps help in catching the killer? How will this so-called doctor-patient confidentiality benefit the murdered girl?"

The doctor shut his eyes for a second and then said: "I'm sorry! I was speaking without thinking. Of course you need to know as much detail about the victim as you can get. It is not for me to decide what information could be relevant – that is for you to decide!"

"Glad to see that you understand – now can you give some more details of Anamika's recent medical problems?"

Srivastava cleared his throat and replied: "Devesh and Sujata Malhotra do not know about this. Nor does Aradhana. I don't think that Rajat knows either. Anamika had sworn me to secrecy. Anamika had visited my clinic a few weeks ago for a pregnancy test, which turned out to be negative…"

***

14

Political and Media Pressure

"So, Anamika Malhotra had a secret lover!" observed Detective Inspector Ramesh Uppal, while carefully steering the police jeep over the narrow road, that led to the orphanage located in the hills touching Gurgaon, where the murdered girl had worked.

"This is a very interesting lead that we've received – one that could have direct relevance to the crime – but I have no idea, yet, how we will identify this mysterious lover," responded Avinash Sharma with some exasperation. He frowned thoughtfully at the passing trees and straightened the tip of his police cap with his baton.

"Dr Srivastava indicated that Anamika's parents and her sister and brother had no knowledge of this boyfriend and lover..."

"This we need to verify – we cannot go just by the doctor's opinion," said Avinash. "When we return to the Malhotra house we should question the family about this aspect of Anamika's life."

Ramesh deftly avoided banging the jeep into a passing cow and observed: "The brother is another mysterious character – he could not be contacted by the family in the early hours of the morning. They could only inform him of his sister's death when he finally called himself. Where had he disappeared to?"

"Good question!" agreed Avinash. "This fellow Rajat Malhotra needs checking out. It'll be interesting to meet him!"

Avinash's cellphone buzzed. He checked out the number on the screen. The caller was his superior officer, the Commissioner of Gurgaon Police, Rajender Saxena. He took the call. "Yes, sir!"

Avinash listened for a while and then commented: "I understand, sir! I'll try to wrap it up as fast as I can. It's very early in the investigation to arrive at any conclusion – but we have some thoughts…"

He listened again and then responded: "I'll return to the Malhotra house well in time for the press conference, sir. Right now, I'm headed for the orphanage where Anamika Malhotra used to work – her sister told us that Anamika had been investigating what she thought were some suspicious activities in the charitable childcare organization, which runs this orphanage. This is one lead I cannot ignore."

He listened again, his face grim, and then said: "Certainly, sir! I understand the pressure. We'll make this investigation our top priority."

As the Commissioner cut the connection, Avinash looked at

Ramesh ruefully and said: "The Prime Minister's Office has been making inquiries about the progress in the case." He shook his head and continued: "The poor girl Anamika's body is not yet cold and already the heavyweights of the country are leaning on us for a quick resolution of the mystery behind her death, thanks to her father's stature and connections. We have some difficult days ahead of us…"

"What's this about a press conference?" asked Ramesh, as the walls of the orphanage came into sight in the distance.

"The media has arrived in full force outside the Malhotra residence," replied Avinash. "They want a statement from the police on the progress of the investigation. Devesh Malhotra immediately called up Commissioner Saxena. The chief is now camping at the Malhotra house. He has promised the assembled media a press statement in the afternoon. He wants us back by then – with some idea of what to tell the press!"

"That's a tough call," sympathized Ramesh. "What – "

He was cut off mid sentence by Avinash Sharma, who suddenly shouted: "Stop the jeep!"

As a highly surprised Ramesh braked and brought the vehicle to a screeching halt, he saw his superior officer jump out and rush into the bushes, by the side of the narrow road. The Detective Superintendent returned to the jeep looking disheveled. He was holding tightly two frightened looking small boys. Both boys looked no more than six or seven years of age.

"I saw them jump down from the wall of the orphanage," said Avinash, slightly out of breath. "That's why I gave chase. I think they were running away from the orphanage!"

Ramesh got out of the jeep from the driver's side and came over to where Avinash was standing with the small boys. "Now why would they want to do that?" he asked, scratching his head, as one of the small boys began to cry.

***

15

The Orphanage

"I am afraid such incidents do occur once in a while," said the silver haired man, in the silk kurta pajama ensemble, with a dark brown shawl draped elegantly around his shoulders. "These children come to us after having faced all sorts of trauma at a very early age. This makes some of them very unstable. It takes time to settle them."

"And what happens to those who run away successfully?" asked Ramesh Uppal. The President of Save the Children in Distress Society looked slightly uncomfortable. "All attempts are made to trace the runaways – but sometimes in vain," answered Rama Prasad Aggarwal, adjusting his shawl a bit self consciously. "We of course lodge a police complaint and also inform the Child Welfare Department of the State of Haryana, under whose jurisdiction we operate all our three orphanages."

Avinash Sharma looked out of the large window of the sparsely but comfortably furnished office and stared at the small children playing or sitting around in the grassy compound of the orphanage. The children looked happy enough – and the lady attendants supervising them looked quite efficient. He turned back to Aggarwal. "We have come to you this morning in connection with a young lady who used to work here – Anamika Malhotra," he said.

Rama Prasad Aggarwal smiled. "Anamika still works here. She's a very sweet and caring girl. She manages the administration of this particular orphanage, but also takes time to interact with the children. She is very concerned with their welfare."

Detective Superintendent Avinash Sharma cleared his throat and said: "Anamika Malhotra is dead. She was murdered early this morning."

Aggarwal turned pale. His hands began to shake. Avinash and Ramesh were closely watching his reaction to the news of Anamika's murder – and they both realized that they were either witnessing genuine shock or were in the presence of a very good actor.

"What-what did you just say? Anamika has been murdered?"

"Yes, Mr Aggarwal," responded Avinash – and recounted the details as briefly and quickly as possible.

Ramesh stared hard. Beads of sweat had appeared on the forehead of Aggarwal. His hands were shaking uncontrollably. And then he noticed the right wrist of the President of Save the

Children in Distress Society. His eyes widened and he quickly looked in the direction of his superior officer. Yes, Avinash had also noticed the beads of sweat. And he had also observed, on Aggarwal's right-wrist, a yellow colored plastic wristband with the words "A Second Chance" written in red letters....

A similar yellow colored plastic wristband had been found by the police teams scouring the grounds of the Malhotra mansion, just a few hours after Anamika's murder.

Before either police officer could react to these observations, Aggarwal picked up the receiver of the intercom instrument and spoke softly into it. He was summoning somebody. Avinash and Ramesh steeled themselves for the unexpected.

The wait was only for about half a minute or so. The door of the office opened and two people stepped inside.

One of the two people was a woman in her mid forties. Dressed in a sober green saree, the dark haired woman had a firm no-nonsense look about her. Her thick spectacles made her look slightly older than her years. She was evidently a member of the staff as – she too wore, on her right wrist, a similar wristband with the same words in red. Avinash and Ramesh realized that their eyes were now automatically gravitating to the right wrists of those they were meeting in the orphanage...

The second member was a young man in his mid thirties. He was a giant – at least six feet four. His slightly scarred face was expressionless. This man looked out of place in the premises of a charitable organization, felt Avinash Sharma.

"Rani Suri is our Executive Director," introduced Aggarwal. "She is the senior most official of our organization. "Surinder Mishra is our Director of Programmes." He turned to the officials and said, his voice shaking slightly: "These police officers have just now informed me that Anamika was murdered this morning!"

Rani Suri and Surinder Mishra looked shocked. Avinash and Ramesh stared hard at them. Was the shock genuine?

They had good reason to entertain doubts. The right wrist of the Director of Programmes, Surinder Mishra, carried no yellow plastic wristband. Had it fallen off and been lost by the wearer in the Malhotra mansion grounds early this morning?

The police officers had made another observation, to fuel their very rapidly mounting suspicions. Among the many items that had been found by the police teams, had been an inexpensive gent's wristwatch in surprisingly good condition, indicating that it had not been lying around in the grass for too long. There was no wristwatch visible on either arm of Surinder Mishra...

***

16

Suspects

Two very thoughtful police officers drove back to the Malhotra mansion, from the orphanage located in the hills through which the Gurgaon-Faridabad road traversed like a ribbon. They had refrained from discussing with Aggarwal the late Anamika's alleged suspicions pertaining to the working of the Society. They had decided that this organization's Director of Programmes, at least, could be added to the list of suspects in the murder investigation – in addition to the mysterious lover of the dead girl. Even Aggarwal needed closer investigation – as did the affairs of the Save the Children in Distress Society.

As Detective Inspector Ramesh Uppal navigated the police jeep swiftly along the winding road towards the Millennium City, as Gurgaon is popularly known, his superior officer dialed his cellphone and spoke to police headquarters. "I need a detailed report on the number of runaways from the three orphanages of Save the Children in Distress Society," he instructed a member of his staff. "I also want to know how many runaways were found and returned to the orphanages – and whether any of these children gave reasons for running away."

Detective Superintendent Avinash Sharma had another concrete request: "Get me as complete a rundown as you can on the background of the President, Executive Director and Director Programmes of Save the Children in Distress Society," he instructed his subordinate over the phone. He gave the assistant the three names.

As the police jeep entered the wide road that led to the palatial house owned by the tycoon Devesh Malhotra, Ramesh slowed the vehicle down to almost a standstill and looked at Avinash with some trepidation.

The road in front of the house was completely blocked by television crews and press reporters. More than a dozen mobile television filming unit vehicles lined each side of the road. Each van represented one leading TV channel or the other. The huge contingent of press reporters from the national and local newspapers and their accompanying cameramen crowded outside the main gates of the mansion. They were prevented from crashing through the imposing gates and invading the house by a large battery of policemen and private security guards.

Avinash sprang to action. He quickly spoke into his cellphone, issuing commands. The policemen at the gates of the Malhotra mansion reacted, as they received the instructions from the police inspector, who received the call from Detective Superintendent Avinash Sharma. They moved forward and physically parted the crowd of reporters and cameramen in front of the gate. Ramesh revved up the engine of the jeep and sped forward – driving through the passage that the policemen had created. The gates of the mansion briefly swung open and Ramesh drove the jeep into the driveway, unmindful of shouts from the journalists for comments and statements. The TV cameras whirred and captured the entrance of the police jeep into Devesh Malhotra's house – followed by the firm closing of the gates. The TV cameras and crew focused their bright lights on their respective reporters. The TV anchors and reporters, make-up on their faces and microphones in their hands, spoke brightly and earnestly into the cameras, speculating on the sudden arrival of the police and the secrets that could be revealed during the much awaited press conference that would now surely follow.

Inside the house, Avinash and Ramesh finally came face-to-face with Devesh Malhotra's eldest child – his son Rajat Malhotra.

***

17

Lines of Investigation

Rajat Malhotra was twenty eight years old. He was a couple of inches taller than his father. He had an athletic and slightly muscular build. He carried himself well – his bearing was that of a combat soldier, disciplined yet adaptable and agile. And yes, he shared the Malhotra family's good fortune in good looks. He was dark haired, handsome and smart.

Avinash Sharma found something dangerous lurking in Rajat Malhotra's eyes. His experienced eyes told him that this son of Devesh Malhotra had a mind and will of his own and could, perhaps, be reckless and ruthless in certain circumstances.

Right now, Rajat Malhotra was looking shocked, devastated and very angry all at the same time. Accompanied by his sister Aradhana, Rajat confronted the two police officers in the main drawing room.

"Any leads to my sister's murderer?" he asked Avinash.

Avinash shook his head. "Nothing concrete yet," he answered. "We are following up on some possibilities, but its early days yet – give us some time."

"Early days!" exclaimed Rajat Malhotra belligerently. "The murderer simply broke into our house, brutally killed my sister and just disappeared and you have no clue more than half a day after the event! What kind of security can citizens of this country expect from its police?"

Avinash was about to retort that a platoon of private security guards had not been able to protect Anamika in her own house against the determined killer, but then thought better of it. The elder brother was apparently overcome with grief – a concession had to be allowed for his state of mind in such tragic circumstances.

The Commissioner of Gurgaon Police, Rajender Saxena, was also present in the room. He intervened. "The police will do all they can to find the killer of your sister, Mr Rajat Malhotra," he told the grieving young man. "Detective Superintendent Avinash Sharma is one of our best officers. He has a formidable reputation for solving difficult crimes. Give him some time – there will be positive results soon." Rajender Saxena then turned to Avinash Sharma and said: "We need to go over the points we will be sharing with the press…"

The three police officers excused themselves and stepped out into the garden. Devesh Malhotra was still closeted with his wife Sujata in their bedroom. The smaller children were being cared for by the maids in a television room, somewhere on the second floor of the house.

Avinash quickly briefed the Police Commissioner on the findings of the day. Rajender Saxena looked concerned. "Both the lines of investigation that you are working on appear positive – but the consequences of a premature announcement could be disastrous..." he remarked.

"You are very right, sir," replied Avinash. "The fact that Anamika had a lover is not something we can broadcast to the world at the moment. The boyfriend, whoever he is, may be completely innocent and uninvolved in the crime. The Malhotra's will not appreciate their daughter's – and their own – reputation being compromised by a public announcement of Anamika's pregnancy test. We also can make no public declaration of our suspicions pertaining to the officials of Save the Children in Distress Society. The affairs of the society and the background of the three top officials are being investigated, based on our suspicions – but even our suspicions are based on hypothesis and conjecture and not on any facts..."

"We will have to make a non-committal statement to the press but we will still have to indicate some forward movement," observed Rajender Saxena, his brow furrowed. "This is an extremely high profile case involving a very influential family. The Prime Minister's Office and the Home Ministry are breathing down my neck for quick results – we have to keep up a certain momentum and also make positive noises to the media."

"I'm sure you will take care of that, sir, for the moment," responded Avinash. "In the meantime, I will need the full resources of the Gurgaon Police Department at my disposal to be able to fully explore all possible leads in double quick time..."

"You will have unrestricted access to all personnel and departments. I will also ensure full support from all Central Government agencies."

"And I need to have a detailed meeting quickly with Aradhana Malhotra regarding the allegations she was making, of suspicious activities in one of her father's companies – the one she was working in. The death threats she and her sister had received must be investigated quickly – this is one lead that is sure to take us to the killer..."

***

18

Press Conference

The press conference was a disaster.

Under instructions from the Commissioner of Gurgaon Police, Rajender Saxena, a small stage had been erected by the police personnel, just outside the gates of the Malhotra mansion, a little to one side so that there was enough space, to allow entry into the house complex, to the many dignitaries and friends and relatives who had begun to arrive, to express their condolences and share in the grief of the mourning family.

An excited murmer spread amongst the representatives of the media as they spotted the three police officers, emerge from behind the large gates of the house and mount the makeshift stage. They sat down on the three chairs that had been provided for them, the Police Commissioner in the centre.

Police personnel manned both the ends of the road leading

to the house, diverting traffic and ensuring that visitors to the house parked their vehicles on the side roads and walked to the Malhotra mansion.

The television crews got to work in right earnest – shining bright lights on the police officers and setting in motion their expensive and high-tech cameras. The engineers camping inside the mobile TV vans checked their instruments and screens. The press and TV reporters piled up their microphones on the small table in front of the police officers to ensure that their every word was caught on tape. Both TV and still cameramen tried to capture the three policemen in their lenses in such a manner that the mansion could also be seen in the background. In the absence of any member of the Malhotra family, it was the house that was the focus of every camera angle for the moment, besides, of course, the police officers.

Rajender Saxena cleared his throat and spoke. A hush fell on the assembled press reporters and cameramen as he described the circumstances in which the unfortunate Anamika was murdered and how her stepmother, Sujata Malhotra, had seen the masked killer just as he had completed his gruesome business. A wave of sympathy for the murdered girl and her devastated stepmother passed, like a tsunami wave, over the assembled media representatives. Later on, many of the reporters would build on the 'what if' story – 'what if' Sujata Malhotra had not gone back to sleep after she had first been awakened by the sound of breaking glass; 'what if' she had been accompanied by the security guards of the house when she had entered her stepdaughter's bedroom. Would the murder have been prevented? Would the murderer have been caught?

The more sensationalists amongst the publications would later also dwell upon the stepmother – step daughter relationship and speculate on its implications, touching but not quite crossing the limits of libelous and scandalous inferences. The thought that the stepmother had not done quite enough to prevent the tragedy would however, remain floating in certain quarters, causing deep anguish in the Malhotra household.

The Police Commissioner finished his summation of events and the reporters scrambled to get in their questions.

How did the killer manage to break into the house so easily?

How did the killer escape so easily?

Surely some telltale signs would have been left behind by the murderer – if such clues had been discovered, what were they?

What details had been found in Anamika Malhotra's life history and recent activities that could throw light on the possible motivation behind the murder?

Was there a possibility that there could be a political angle to the murder – considering that the dead girl's father was a close confidant of the Prime Minister?

Would the Prime Minister be attending the cremation?

Rajender Saxena could provide no answers. There was no way

he would be divulging details of Anamika's alleged lover or the suspicions relating to her last employer. Nor would he be revealing to the media and the public, so early in the investigation process, the death threats to the twin sisters. After a few "no comments" or "more details will be given after investigations have made some progress" he realized the futility of further attempts to temporarily satiate a news and newsbyte hungry press – and called off the press briefing.

The three police officers hastily re-entered the house to try and find an opportunity to question Sujata Malhotra, the only eyewitness to the murder, while the press reporters continued throwing their questions, unmindful that the Police Commissioner had brought the briefing to a close.

As the gates of the Malhotra mansion closed behind the three officers, the TV reporters turned to face their cameras and began to talk earnestly about a police force that appeared to be unable to cope with the current crisis and made speculation, on camera, about dark political forces that could be behind the tragedy. The press reporters filed similar stories.

The Gurgaon Police had come into the national spotlight – poor Anamika's brutal murder had become the hot subject of a media circus…

***

19

The Soul Departs

Anamika Malhotra's cremation was attended by a host of political and business leaders of the country – as befitting the daughter of a leading industrialist, who was also a member of the Economic Advisory Council that was chaired by the Prime Minister of India.

Her cremation was also covered in detail by all leading newspapers and television channels of the country not just because of her illustrious lineage but also because of the tragic manner of her death. Anamika was news in death if not in life.

The cremation took place in Delhi. All roads leading to the cremation grounds had been cordoned off – to ensure security for the dignitaries who would attend and also to facilitate the smooth movement and parking of the almost hundred or so vehicles of the attendees.

The Prime Minister sent his Minister In-charge of the Prime

Minister's Office (PMO) to represent him. The Home Minister was present at the cremation, as was the Minister of Finance. Devesh Malhotra's stature and position were greatly emphasized and reinforced at his daughter's cremation – if such emphasis and reinforcement were actually needed. Devesh Malhotra, himself, was too overtaken by grief to care for or notice this.

Anamika's body had been repaired after the mandatory autopsy and returned to the family by the police and hospital authorities on the night of the same day she had been killed. She now bore no signs of the brutality that had been inflicted on her body at the time of her death. Anamika had lain peacefully, wrapped up completely in white on the floor of the main lobby of the mansion, in which she had grown up and whose walls had resounded with the sounds of her laughter first as a bubbly child, then a gawky teenager and then as a beautiful and lively young lady.

The immediate family and other family members and relatives grieved all night. Towards morning, the women washed Anamika's body, applied sandal paste and turmeric and decorated it with items of her jewellery they knew she was fond of.

At the cremation grounds, the funeral pyre had been kept ready using the best of sandalwood that had been available in the city. No expense would be spared to ensure the smooth transition of the tragically departed young girl's soul from her physical body to the astral world. As the body was gently placed on top of the pyre, a loud wailing was heard from the women in the crowd.

Everyone's eyes – were moist with tears as Devesh Malhotra, supported by his eldest son, stepped forward to perform a task he had never, till twenty four hours ago, ever dreamt that he would need to perform in his life – light his daughter's funeral pyre.

As the flames leaped towards the sky, the priests began chanting, in a hypnotic monotone, the Vedic mantras designed to lessen the pain the soul suffers, as it separates itself from the now dead physical body, to which it has developed an attachment while travelling through life on earth. As the priests urged the soul to begin its peaceful and smooth transition to the astral world, the Vedic chants also began performing their task of providing psychological healing to the mourners.

Some mourners, however, refused to kill their grief. They would carry the flame of their sorrow and anger until the dead girl had been avenged.

Detective Superintendent Avinash Sharma stood amongst the crowd of mourners with his head bowed. In all his professional life as a policeman, he had never allowed his emotions to overtake his technical job of investigating unnatural deaths and bringing the perpetrator of such violent acts to justice. But the brutal killing of the young girl had moved him deeply. He vowed once again that he would track down the girl's killer, come what may.

In the gathering of women, a little away from the area of the burning pyre, Aradhana Malhotra mourned her twin sister with deep intensity. She knew that she would know no peace on this earth until her sister's terrible death had been avenged.

Right next to the pyre, in his now dirty and soiled white cotton kurta pajama, stood Rajat Malhotra, his right hand gripping his father's shoulder in a gesture of solidarity and support. The smoke was thick and burnt the eyes – but that was not the reason why Rajat's eyes were wet. As his tears ran down his cheeks, he locked his eyes with Avinash Sharma across his sister's pyre. There was a challenge in his eyes that the police officer could not miss, even at that distance. If the police did their job in double quick time, it would be good – else the brother would have to take things into his own hands...

***

20

Kathmandu, Nepal

Hotel Himalayan View lived up to its name. The finest hotel in Kathmandu was located on the outskirts of the capital city of Nepal and commanded a magnificent view of the towering, snowcapped Himalayan Mountains. Normally, the beautiful white mountains of the Himalayan ranges were hidden from the residents of the Kathmandu valley by clouds and mist and the after effects of air pollution. However, the location of Hotel Himalayan View had been well chosen – the hotel had been constructed ten years previously at a spot from where, mysteriously, was available a clear and mesmerizing view of the snowy Himalayas most days of the year. There was no haze over the mountains visible from this spot. The owner had only one boast: He did not go to Kathmandu – rather, Kathmandu, in fact the whole world, came to his hotel, to drink in the view of the majestic Himalayas and also to gamble freely and happily in the hotel's plush casino.

Four days after his sister's cremation. Rajat Malhotra strode into the ground floor casino of Hotel Himalayan View at 6 pm in the evening.

The evening's revelries were just kicking off, but already the twelve thousand square feet casino was full of gamblers and party animals. There were crowds of merry makers in each of the casino's distinct and separate sections – the slot machines area, the hall where the card tables were located, the section where the roulette games were played, the bar and the sitting area in front of the small stage where trained dancers, Nepali boys in tight pants and Nepali girls in short skirts, were dancing, rather gyrating, to popular Bollywood film music.

Rajat Malhotra had not come to gamble – he headed straight for the bar area.

Mini skirted Nepali girls carrying trays of complimentary cigarettes accosted him as he navigated his way to the bar. But Rajat was not interested. The bar was crowded – all the bar stools were occupied. As per Nepali casino business tradition, not just the cigarettes but even the beverages, both alcoholic and non-alcoholic, were free. Unlimited snacks were also on the house. This encouraged the gamblers to relax and spend quality time in the casino. Experience – and research – has shown that such investments have paid off with bumper profits for casino owners. High on free drinks, free cigarettes, free snacks and free entertainment, many thousands of gamblers have gambled away fortunes and more to the 'house', in night long binges in the casinos of Kathmandu…

Rajat found a corner table and made himself comfortable. He surveyed his surroundings.

Loud voices could be heard from the centre of the bar area. The owner of the hotel was present and was holding forth.

He was a large, fat, balding man called Anoop Puri. He was an Indian citizen – and was reputed to be one of the top four mafia and underworld dons of India. He was also the casino king of Nepal.

Anoop Puri looked happy. He had clearly not yet been informed, of the theft of his twenty parcels of cash stored in the underground vault of the cargo terminal of Mumbai's Chattrapati Shivaji International Airport, less than a week ago. The airport authorities had been advised to keep quiet about the theft by the Indian Aviation Ministry, to give a chance to the police to track down the thieves without media pressure and pressure from a worried owner. The Aviation Ministry had been guided to do this by the Indian Home Ministry. Neither the airport authorities nor the Aviation Ministry knew what the Home Ministry knew – that the twenty parcels, that had been stolen in that daring predawn heist, contained untraceable money to the tune of about three million dollars, taken from collections at several casinos run by

Anoop Puri and his Indian mafia in the capital city of Nepal.

They also certainly did not know about the list of candidates that had been hidden in one of the stolen parcels – potential candidates chosen by the mafia to fight elections to the Indian Parliament.

The tip off regarding the cash and the list of names hidden in the parcels had come to the Home Ministry's Intelligence Unit from one of the informers planted in the higher echelons of the Indian underworld. A seizure of the consignment of parcels by the Indian law enforcement agencies would have exposed the informant. Hence the task of taking custody of the parcels, by staging an elaborate heist, was given to the Special Operations Unit (SOU) of the Indian Home Ministry, of which Rajat Malhotra was a key and extremely well trained and ruthless member.

If and when Anoop Puri and the other leaders of the Indian mafia got to know of their loss, it would be assumed that the parcels had been stolen by a highly professional gang of thieves…

At this moment, raids were being conducted in India in the offices and residences of several of the names mentioned in the mafia list that had been hidden in the parcels. Based on the evidence of ill-gotten wealth and unlawful activities, that was being gathered, these would-be parliamentarians were being taken into custody by the law enforcement agencies. Another devious plan of the Indian underworld to infiltrate Indian government and polity had been foiled….

But the mafia kingpins were still around and active – they would eventually go on to hatch other conspiracies. For a permanent solution to the problem, they needed to be exposed.

Rajat waited.

A young lady sitting at a table next to Anoop Puri's began to get agitated. He had a preference for pungent cigars – and he was puffing away at one right now, while sipping his wine and cracking jokes with his cronies. The smoke from the cigar was wafting in the direction of the young lady at the next table. It appeared to be disturbing her.

She began to cough and wave her hands in front of her face in a vain attempt to ward off the irritating cigar fumes.

Anoop Puri appeared not to notice these signs of discomfort. He continued to puff away at his thick cigar. Someone at his table cracked a joke and he broke into a roar of laughter. His belly heaved like a tidal wave as he laughed and puffed away at his cigar.

The young lady turned to him. "Could you extinguish your cigar, please?" she said as she continued to cough. "The smoke is hurting my throat and eyes."

At first, Anoop Puri appeared not to hear. The young lady's voice must have been loud enough, since the three companions at his table fell silent at her words. Anoop Puri took a drag at his cigar.

This time, she spoke more firmly and loudly. "Please extinguish your cigar. It's creating a problem for me."

Men sitting at a few nearby tables stiffened and looked in the direction of the young lady and her male companion, who had said nothing so far but who was also beginning to show signs of joining this one-sided conversation. The men surrounding the don's table were his bodyguards – and were trained to become alert at the slightest sign of trouble. They stared sternly at this presumptuous young lady and her companion.

Like an ocean liner turning in mid-ocean, Anoop Puri slowly swerved in his chair to look at the young lady who had asked him to extinguish his cigar. He studied the girl for a moment and then said softly: "This cigar will be extinguished when it is finished and not before. If you have a problem with my smoking, then move your pretty bottom to another chair at another table." Having made his point, he turned back to his cronies. His bodyguards at the nearby tables relaxed visibly.

The male companion now spoke: "Is this the way to speak to a lady?"

A hush fell over the bar area. Everyone turned to look at Anoop Puri. How would he react to such impertinence?

Anoop Puri's face flushed a deep red. His eyes blazed. He looked at a nearby table occupied by some of his bodyguards. His eyes flashed their message.

One of them got to his feet and strode over to the young lady. "Get out of this hotel, right now!" he ordered, looking directly at the male companion.

As all eyes focused on the drama being enacted in the centre of the bar area, several men moved from various corners of the casino and stood casually around. A couple of men from one corner of the casino came over and stood by the table occupied by Anoop Puri. The young lady and her male companion got slowly to their feet.

Rajat Malhotra also got to his feet.

As Rajat began to walk towards the tables in the centre of the bar area where the drama was being enacted, the young lady, who had began the tense exchange of words, began to cough loudly.

Concerned, her companion put a hand on her shoulder.

The bodyguard of the mafia don, who had ordered the couple to leave the hotel stood nonplussed – not quite knowing how to react to the young lady's coughing fit.

Anoop Puri ignored the couple and continued to puff away at his cigar. But all laughter had disappeared from his table to be replaced by tension.

Rajat Malhotra walked past the coughing lady, her companion and the threatening bodyguard and came to a halt at the table occupied by Anoop Puri. He towered over the mafia leader who continued to smoke nonchalantly.

"Didn't you hear the young lady?" Rajat demanded. "Kindly extinguish your cigar."

Several things happened simultaneously at this extremely unexpected intervention. The bodyguards of Anoop Puri at the nearby tables all jumped to their feet – and were immediately gunned down, in a blaze of noise and smoke, by the men who had come over to the scene from other corners of the casino. As the gunshots rang out, the young lady pulled out a pistol from her handbag and shot the bodyguard who had threatened her. As he fell, her companion pulled out a gun and shot one of Puri's table companions in the face. Two other men standing near the mafia leader's table shot dead the other two cronies of Anoop Puri.

In less than thirty seconds, nine bodyguards of Anoop Puri and his three cronies lay dead on the floor of the bar area of the casino of Hotel Himalayan View. The air was thick with smoke that had emanated from the blazing guns. As women screamed and men shouted, Rajat Malhotra pulled out his gun and shot Anoop Puri. The bullet crashed through the front of his skull and shredding his brain. Anoop Puri did not know he had been shot until he was dead.

Rajat, accompanied by the young lady who had started all the commotion, her companion and the many gunmen who had killed Anoop Puri's bodyguards, then calmly walked out of the casino and the hotel. They got into several vehicles, that were waiting at the main entrance of the hotel with engines running and drivers in position – and drove away to a nearby air force base where a private plane was waiting for them.

There was no Nepalese policeman in sight. There would be no obstruction at the air force base. Indo-Nepal co-operation had just recorded another success…

***

21

Digging into Backgrounds

Detective Superintendent Avinash Sharma studied the reports in amazement. The background checks that he had ordered on the President, Executive Director and Director Programmes of Save the Children in Distress Society had thrown up several surprises. Ten years ago, the President Aggarwal, had served a year in jail on tax evasion charges.

Eight years ago, the Director Programmes, Surinder Mishra, had led a gang of kidnappers and extortionists in western UP. He had been caught and found guilty in relation to two cases of kidnapping – and had served a jail term of five years.

The report on the Executive Director was even more stunning – there was no record available anywhere pertaining to her background, prior to joining the employment of the charitable organization that operated three orphanages in Haryana. It was as if the lady called Rani Suri, had never existed till about a year ago.

Avinash passed on the reports to his junior colleague Detective Inspector Ramesh Uppal and watched his face express amazement, shock and disbelief almost simultaneously.

"Do you think that the Save the Children in Distress Society could be a front for something shady – some illegal activity of some kind?" asked Ramesh.

"Judging by the backgrounds of the senior most officials of this so-called charitable organization, this is an eminently feasible possibility!" remarked Avinash Sharma.

"So, do we pull them in for questioning?" asked Ramesh hopefully.

Avinash shook his head. "That would be going too fast. You can't damn a person because of their past. They may have reformed…" His face expressed his own disbelief at his statement.

"Shall we put a twenty four hour watch on the three orphanages of the Society?" offered Ramesh.

"Yes. That should be done immediately – but clandestinely. Rama Prasad Aggarwal and his cronies should not get to know that the police are keeping a watch on them. They'll never expose themselves and their dubious activities, if any, if they know that they are under police watch." Avinash became thoughtful. "It seems that Anamika Malhotra was right to harbour suspicions about the true activities of the organization she was working for. The question we need to find an answer to is: how much and what did she find out?"

"And did Aggarwal and his cronies know that Anamika was investigating their clandestine activities, if any? Because if they did know this, then we have a motive for her murder…" concluded Ramesh.

"Yes. This line of investigation is warming up. It may explain the presence of the Save the Children in Distress Society trademark yellow wristband and the wristwatch, in the grounds of the Malhotra mansion, just after the murder. Both items were missing from the arm of Surinder Mishra!" remarked Avinash.

Both police detectives became grave. They were contemplating the implications of all that they had just discussed. "Do you think Surinder Mishra is the killer?" asked Ramesh.

"Circumstantial evidence appears to indicate this – but we need hard evidence," responded Avinash. "This is a very high profile case and any mistake would be magnified by the huge media interest. The reputation of Gurgaon police will be greatly damaged if we make wrong arrests. We must be absolutely certain of our evidence before we make any arrests."

"Surinder Mishra's background certainly makes him a possible suspect!" observed Ramesh. "He's served a jail term of five years for kidnapping – he's certainly no angel!"

Avinash's head jerked up. His eyes flashed. "Of course!" he exclaimed. "That's the line of investigation we must pursue. Surinder Mishra was a kidnapper. This is something we must explore – where are the children in the orphanages coming from?"

***

22

The Children

Avinash Sharma had asked his staff at Gurgaon Police headquarters for a report on the number of runaways from the three orphanages. He also wanted to know how many runaways had been found and returned – and whether any of these children had given reasons for running away. This report was as revealing as had been the background check on the officials of the Society.

Children living in the orphanages did not appear to be happy, if one were to judge by the number and frequency of runaways.

Each of them, located in Gurgaon, Panipat and Karnal, housed around thirty orphans at any point of time. For the last three years, which was the duration covered by the reports prepared by Avinash Sharma's staff, there had had been an average of three runaways per year from the Gurgaon orphanage, two from Panipat and two from Karnal. This appeared to be a very large percentage of unhappy children – considering the relatively few children each orphanage housed.

"The runaways are all very young," commented Ramesh, after studying the report. "They were all aged around six or seven at the time of their escape." He looked thoughtfully at Avinash. "The two boys you caught running away from the orphanage were also this age, weren't they?"

"Yes," responded Avinash. "And there is a reason for that!" He pointed to another report in his hand. "I had asked for a detailed report on the organization, operations and project details of the Society. You will be surprised to note that the maximum age of children in these orphanages is seven…"

"Where do the children go after the age of seven?" asked Ramesh.

"That's precisely the question that needs to be answered by the officials!" observed Avinash. "I have a feeling that this matter of high number of runaways and disappearance of children from the orphanages after age six or seven is connected with the suspicious activities that Anamika was investigating – ."

"And hence connected with her murder!" exclaimed Ramesh. He pondered for a while and then asked: "What were the reasons that the children gave for running away?"

Avinash looked grim. "That's the strangest part of it all – there is no record anywhere of any investigation having been done on the reasons behind the children running away."

"But how is that possible?" queried Ramesh. "The Child Welfare Department would have insisted on this. They can cancel an orphanage's license to operate if these regulatory requirements and self-audit processes are not followed..."

"I smell connivance," stated Avinash grimly. "The more we investigate, the more it appears that there is serious hanky panky going on behind the façade of a charity. And some corrupt government officials in the Child Welfare Department are facilitating this. We must find out what is going on quickly!"

"Shall I call for a jeep?" asked Detective Inspector Ramesh.

"Yes. Let's go to the Gurgaon orphanage and ourselves interview the two runaways..."

An hour later, the two arrived at the gates of the orphanage. They were received by an extremely worried looking Aggarwal.

"Nice to see you again, Superintendent," he said, looking uneasy. "What can I do for you?"

Avinash came straight to the point. "I would like to meet the two boys I caught while they were trying to run away."

Aggarwal looked distinctly unhappy. "Any particular reason for this request?" he asked, avoiding eye contact.

Avinash was in no mood to soft pedal. "I want to meet the boys. Please call them."

A lady's voice spoke behind him. Avinash whirled around to face Rani Suri, the Executive Director, "I'm afraid those two boys are not here," announced the lady.

Avinash and Ramesh stared at Rani Suri in amazement. "Where are the boys?" asked Ramesh quickly.

"They have been taken to our Panipat orphanage," replied Rani Suri, her face expressionless.

"Why?" asked Avinash bluntly.

"Since they appeared unhappy here, we felt that a change of environment would help them settle down better," she said.

Avinash turned to face Aggarwal. "Is this standard procedure?" he inquired.

"Uh – yes, most of the time," he responded, staring at Rani.

Avinash and Ramesh looked at each other – and both police officers had the same thought in their minds: were the two boys in some kind of danger?

Avinash decided to escalate matters. "Can you get the boys back here by tomorrow?" he asked, "We definitely would like to meet them. We can go to the Panipat orphanage also, if necessary."

"That will not be necessary," quickly intervened Rani. "We'll get the boys back here. I'll telephone the orphanage at Panipat and speak to Surinder Mishra."

"Your Director Programmes is also at the Panipat orphanage?" asked Avinash.

"He's the person who has taken the boys there," she replied.

Avinash and Ramesh again looked at each other. This piece of information greatly heightened their worry about the two missing boys...

***

23

Confession

The two police officers did not return to the Gurgaon Police headquarters.

Instead they headed for Panipat.

Ramesh deftly raced the police jeep through the Gurgaon-Mehrauli Road into New Delhi's Ring Road. They headed for the GT Road – which would take them to the city of Panipat, about two hours drive from the Delhi-Haryana border.

They had not informed anyone of their intention to visit the Panipat orphanage – so the telephone call which Detective Superintendent Avinash Sharma received from Aggarwal, was a surprise.

Avinash saw the number flashing on his mobile screen and motioned Ramesh to slow down the jeep and park to one side of the Ring Road. This was a traffic violation, but the detectives knew that the Delhi police would turn a blind eye to this minor misdemeanor by their colleagues from across the border…

As Ramesh parked the jeep on one side of the road, Avinash answered Aggarwal's phone call.

"I assume you are on your way to the Panipat orphanage?"

Avinash turned wary. "What makes you assume that?"

"You are not a fool, Superintendent – and neither am I. It is clear to me that you have some suspicions regarding our Society. You want to meet the runaways – you feel that we have something to hide."

Avinash did not respond. His vast experience told him that the caller was beginning to come apart under some kind of pressure – hence the phone call. He would let the matter unravel by itself.

"I am sure that your suspicions have led you to check our backgrounds – you perhaps know of Surinder Mishra's past crimes…"

Avinash finally reacted: "Do you want to tell me something?"

There was a pause at the other end. Then: "Yes, Superintendent, I want to tell you some facts about Save the Children in Distress Society that may shock you – though you already seem to be harbouring suspicions that all is not above board here."

"So what is the truth?"

"Can you come back to my office now? I would like to tell you the complete truth…"

Avinash Sharma's heart leapt. Was this the breakthrough he

had been waiting for? "My first concern is the safety of the two runaways," he responded, as the Delhi traffic whizzed past their parked jeep. "Are they safe with Surinder Mishra?"

"They are not with him," came the surprising reply. "That was a false statement made by Rani – just to put you off the scent. The boys are not in the Panipat orphanage."

Avinash was puzzled and worried at the same time. "Then where are they?" he asked.

There was a pause. Then: "The boys have been sold off…"

***

24

Retribution

For a moment, Avinash thought he had heard wrong. "What?"

"Yes, Superintendent – that's what we do; we kidnap children and then sell them for adoption. The orphanage work is a cover for our real activities."

Avinash Sharma realized that he would have to get back to the Gurgaon orphanage fast. A phone call in the middle of the road was no way to take a confession. However, he still had one more urgent question to ask. "Are you responsible for Anamika Malhotra's murder?"

"No, no!" shouted Rama Prasad Aggarwal over the phone, "but I think I know who is responsible. I did not know that he would do it – but when you told me of poor Anamika's murder I think I guessed!" After a brief pause, he said: "This is why I am confessing to you – to make it clear that I had no knowledge of the poor girl's murder!"

Avinash was torn between standing there on Delhi's Ring Road and continuing the conversation over the phone or immediately rushing back to the orphanage to take a face-to-face confession. However, before ending the phone call, he just had to know the name on Rama Prasad Aggarwal's lips – he would not have the patience to wait for that...

"Are you trying to tell me that Surinder Mishra killed Anamika Malhotra?"

The answer surprised Avinash Sharma. "No, Surinder Mishra did not kill Anamika."

Avinash Sharma was fast losing patience. "Then who did?"

Amid the roar of the passing traffic, Avinash still heard the sound of a shout at the other end – and then the phone was abruptly disconnected.

Avinash froze. Had Aggarwal been cut off in mid-confession?

Desperately, Avinash re-dialed the last recorded number in his instrument's memory. The phone rang at the other end – and kept ringing...

Avinash lost no further time. It was perhaps too late already. He jumped into the jeep and shouted to a surprised Ramesh: "Take the first u-turn and head back to Gurgaon! We've got to get back to the orphanage!"

Sensing that there was a crisis at hand, Ramesh asked no questions. He ignited the engine with a quick turn of the key and threw the vehicle into gear. As the jeep raced off to seek out the first exit and u-turn on the highway, Avinash dialed the Gurgaon Police Headquarters and ordered for a police convoy to immediately depart for the orphanage in the Aravalli hills.

The next fifty minutes were amongst the tensest in the life of Detective Superintendent Avinash Sharma.

As Ramesh raced the jeep over Ring Road and then Mehrauli-Gurgaon Road without banging into another vehicle or knocking down a pedestrian, Avinash kept re-dialing the landline telephone number of the Gurgaon orphanage. The phone just kept ringing at the other end. This was ominous…

Avinash also telephoned the Inspector leading the police convoy to the Gurgaon orphanage, urging him to speed up. He feared the worst – and shared his fears with his colleague.

Avinash and Ramesh had still not reached the Delhi-Gurgaon border when the police convoy reached the gates of their destination. Avinash got the news over his cellphone.

The police team had needed to break down the door of the office of the President. The door had been locked – from the outside. Rama Prasad Aggarwal had been found inside the room – lying on the floor in a pool of blood…his throat slit.

***

25

Manhunt and Confusion

Rani Suri and Surinder Mishra were not found on the Gurgaon orphanage premises. They had vanished. The directors of the other two orphanages – one in Panipat and one in Karnal – denied any knowledge of their whereabouts. Police teams were dispatched to these orphanages. In the light of the confession made by Rama Prasad Aggarwal, just before his death, regarding the child kidnapping and child trafficking activities of the Save the Children in Distress Society, the orphanage directors were taken into custody. However, Rani and Surinder remained untraceable…

A nationwide manhunt was launched. Airports around the country were put on alert. Railway stations were put under police observation – but this was a mammoth task and not much expectation was placed for results from this initiative.

Meanwhile, the national electronic and print media, laid

siege to the Gurgaon Police Headquarters. They demanded an update – the mysterious murder of the former employer of the dead girl Anamika Malhotra was almost certainly connected with her brutal murder felt the press representatives, and insisted on an immediate briefing.

So did the Prime Minister's Office and the Home Ministry.

Commissioner of Gurgaon Police, Rajender Saxena took a detailed briefing from Detective Superintendent Avinash Sharma and Detective Inspector Ramesh Uppal before scheduling closed door meetings with senior officials of the PMO and the Home Ministry.

"Did Rama Prasad Aggarwal arrange for the killing of Anamika Malhotra?" Rajender Saxena asked Avinash Sharma.

"He denied outright when I asked him."

"But Aggarwal knew who had killed Anamika – is that why he is now dead?"

"Yes – it would appear so. Aggarwal was in a confessional mode when he telephoned me while I was on my way to the Panipat orphanage. He was on the verge of telling me the name of the murderer, I think, when the phone was abruptly disconnected at his end. I think I heard a shout in the background before the phone was cut off..."

"So Surinder Mishra, the previously convicted kidnapper, killed Anamika Malhotra when she began investigating the truth behind the orphanages – and then murdered Aggarwal when he overheard him talking to you on the phone and spilling the beans."

"Aggarwal told me that Anamika's killer was not Surinder Mishra."

"Then who was it? Rani Suri?"

"That's the only other name that I can think of, sir," responded Avinash.

"So the case has been solved, then! Anamika Malhotra began to realize that all was not above board in the organization she was working for. She began investigations – she was probably on the verge of stumbling upon the truth about the kidnapping of children and selling them for adoption. The senior officials felt that she was getting too close to the truth – and decided to do away with her. Aggarwal was probably not a party to the decision to murder the poor girl – but either Surinder Mishra or Rani Suri or both went and did it anyway..."

Ramesh nodded his head while Rajender Saxena was speaking. "The plastic wristband and wristwatch discovered on the grounds of the Malhotra mansion must have fallen from Surinder Mishra's arm that night – while he was running away after being discovered by Sujata Malhotra," contributed Ramesh.

"It was a man that Sujata Malhotra saw in Anamika's bedroom that night, remember?" said Rajender Saxena. "That man must have been Surinder Mishra!"

"But Aggarwal told me very clearly that the killer was not Surinder Mishra, sir!" exclaimed Avinash. "And this makes it difficult to understand why Mishra would kill Aggarwal – who had absolved him of the murder."

Rajender Saxena's face fell. "You are right, Avinash," he admitted. "The killer of Anamika, whose name Aggarwal was about to reveal to you over the phone, was the one who also murdered Aggarwal himself. The killer was not Surinder Mishra since Aggarwal had denied his involvement. So Surinder had no motive to kill him. Yet Anamika Malhotra's killer, if we are to go by Sujata Malhotra's eyewitness account, was a man – this means that it was not Rani Suri. The two – Surinder Mishra and Rani Suri, are absconding, to evade arrest on kidnapping and child trafficking charges – but they are not the killers of Anamika and Aggarwal..." Rajender Saxena looked helplessly at Avinash and asked: "Then who is the killer?"

***

26

More Confusion

Commissioner of Gurgaon Police, Rajender Saxena was forced to give an inconclusive report to the PMO and Home Ministry.

The press were not briefed immediately – first, the three police officers, Rajender Saxena, Avinash and Ramesh, faced an extremely angry father, stepmother, brother and sister of the murdered girl....

The grieving and angry Malhotra family met the police officers at the Gurgaon Police Headquarters.

Devesh Malhotra took charge of the meeting from the very outset. His rugged and handsome face was dark with fury. The three police officers were at the receiving end of the tycoon's anger – the senior rank of the Commissioner of Police counted for nothing to the father of the murdered girl.

"I don't understand why it's taking so long to catch Anamika's killer!" exclaimed Devesh Malhotra angrily. "Now the murderer has gone and killed Aggarwal also – there is a monster on the loose and the police are incapable of catching him!"

"That's not quite correct, Mr Malhotra," responded Rajender Saxena. "The reality behind Save the Children in Distress Society has come to light only because of the efforts of the police..."

"What good has that done?" Devesh Malhotra's eyes were blazing. "The murderer has killed again and disappeared!"

Rajender Saxena spoke firmly. "The good that has been done is that the small children who were kidnapped by Aggarwal and his gang and kept in the orphanages, brainwashed and sold for adoption, will now be restored to their parents. The other officials we have arrested are singing like birds. We are getting details of the couples who have clandestinely bought kids for adoption from Save the Children in Distress Society. We will trace these children and restore them to their parents and families. The gang members have revealed the names of the conniving officials in the Child Welfare Department and other government agencies. These corrupt officials are being taken into custody at this very moment. The orphanages have been handed over to a leading and very credible national level child welfare agency."

"But the murderer of my daughter is still at large!" reminded Devesh Malhotra with emphasis.

"Rani Suri and Surinder Mishra will soon be in our custody," responded Rajender Saxena. "They should, in all probability, know who killed Aggarwal, who was silenced to prevent him from revealing the murderer's name."

Rajat Malhotra now intervened. His handsome face was creased into a deep frown. "You all seem convinced that my sister's killer was not Surinder Mishra," he commented, his eyes moving from Rajender Saxena to Avinash Sharma to Ramesh Uppal. "Since my mother," he looked at Sujata Malhotra, "saw a masked man in Anamika's room, we are ruling out the direct involvement of the woman called Rani Suri – though she may have been a part of the murder conspiracy, if not the actual killer." Rajat looked directly at Avinash and asked: "Was there any other senior official of the Society who was leading their operations – other than Aggarwal, Rani and Surinder Mishra – whom you have not questioned?"

Avinash studied Rajat Malhotra carefully before responding. Was the Malhotra scion leading him into something?

"As far as I know, we have met and questioned all the senior officials of the Society – one of whom is now dead," responded Avinash.

"I suggest you get your act together, Superintendent!" said Rajat with a grim look on his face. "You've left out an important possible suspect from the ambit of your investigations..."

Avinash's face flushed. He was not used to being spoken like this. "What do you mean?" he asked angrily.

Rajat's reply had the impact of shaking the ground beneath Avinash's feet. "You left out the Director for Fundraising from your investigations, Superintendent!" said the Malhotra scion.

As Avinash recoiled at these words, Rajat burst another bomb. "The Society's Director for Fundraising is also the son of Rama Prasad Aggarwal…"

***

27

Missing Suspects

Commissioner of Gurgaon Police Rajender Saxena was the first to react after the initial, stunned silence that had followed this revelation. "How do you know this?" he asked.

"Because I made it my business to know all about the organization that was being investigated by the police for possible involvement in my sister's murder!" was the retort.

It took about a minute for the full meaning of the words to sink in. "How did you come to know that we were investigating Save the Children in Distress Society?" asked Avinash in amazement. "This line of investigation was not public knowledge – it came to light only after the murder of Aggarwal…"

All eyes turned towards the muscular and tough looking young man. Even Rajat's family appeared confused.

Rajat however remained unfazed. "I have my sources,' he

responded simply. "But that is not the point – do not divert this discussion from the fact that the police were completely unaware of the fourth important member of the gang of kidnappers that operated Save the Children in Distress Society!"

There was no arguing with this. "What's the name of Aggarwal's son and where can he be found?" asked Rajender Saxena, fully realizing the oddity of the police asking the victim's brother such a question.

"The name of the Director is Sudesh Aggarwal – Rama Prasad Aggarwal's only son – in fact his only child. He had befriended Anamika and was instrumental in her joining the Society," informed Rajat. "All this I have found out through enquiries I have made on my own." He looked pointedly at Avinash.

An alarm bell rang in Avinash's head. "What do you mean by saying that Sudesh Aggarwal befriended Anamika?" he asked quickly.

At this, Aradhana Malhotra's head jerked up. "What are you implying, Superintendent?" she asked, with an edge to her voice.

Avinash ignored Aradhana but kept looking at her elder brother.

Rajat did not flinch. "Anamika and Sudesh were lovers," he replied.

"What!" Aradhana swiveled around and stared at Rajat in shock and amazement. Her parents did likewise.

It was Avinash who broke the silence. "So Sudesh Aggarwal

is the mysterious boyfriend," he commented.

"You knew that Anamika had a lover?" asked Devesh Malhotra.

In a few crisp sentences, Avinash recounted to the stunned father, mother and sister the revelations made by their neighbour Dr Rajeev Srivastava about Anamika's visit to his clinic a few weeks before her murder, for a pregnancy test which turned out to be negative…

Sujata Malhotra looked completely horrified. "This – this puts a completely new complexion to the case!" she exclaimed. "Was Anamika killed by her lover to hide the relationship?"

"Perhaps not," commented Avinash. "The relationship was probably initiated by Sudesh to bring Anamika on board the Society to give it some credibility. Having the daughter of the PM's Economic Advisor in the employ of Save the Children in Distress Society was a perfect cover for diverting any attention from the actual clandestine activities of the organization. The ploy backfired because Anamika soon became suspicious…"

"Poor poor Anamika!" cried out Aradhana. "That manipulating son-of-a-bitch Sudesh Aggarwal must not be allowed to get away with my sister's murder!"

"None of the gang members will be allowed to get away!" observed Rajender Saxena grimly. "One of them has already paid the price for his crimes. The others will also be punished for their misdeeds."

"When and how Commissioner?" asked Rajat angrily. "It appears to me that they have already made good their escape!"

Detective Superintendent Avinash Sharma could not control his temper any further. "Since you seem to possess resources and information channels far beyond the capabilities of the Gurgaon police, why don't you produce the missing suspects and help us out?" he said bitingly to Rajat.

Devesh Malhotra was about to react to this barb aimed at his son – but Rajat quickly responded before his father could say a word: "I believe that I actually will do that, Superintendent – yes, I will…"

***

28

Taking Action

Dev Dutt Tiwari was unable to hear the voice at the other end.

The noise inside the garage drowned out all sounds coming from his cellphone – he was unable to make out a single word that the caller was speaking.

The noise would not stop. A truck that had met with an accident a few days ago was being fixed. The denting work was creating all the din. The hammering and banging was loud enough to wake the dead – Dev Dutt Tiwari would have to step outside his garage to listen to the words of the caller.

The drug lord of western Uttar Pradesh stepped out of his garage, located in Ghaziabad – the industrial township located on the Delhi UP border – and into the sunlight of the open road. He uttered an oath as he noticed that the mysterious caller had cut the connection. He deliberated whether to call back or not. Then several unexpected events occurred simultaneously…

With a sharp screech of tyres, a Tata Safari SUV braked to a halt next to him. Before Dev Dutt Tiwari could properly register the presence of the huge vehicle barely a few inches away from him, the two doors on the left side were thrown open. The corner of the rear left door hit him squarely on his chest – and he collapsed to the ground. Two of his bodyguards, who had been loitering at the entrance of Dev Dutt Tiwari's Reliable Motors Garage, pulled out pistols from their jacket pockets in a reflex action, born out of many years of training and rough action in the badlands of western UP. The two bodyguards could not, however, put their pistols to any use – they were cut down in a hail of bullets that emerged from the interiors of the Tata Safari SUV.

Simultaneously, two bulky men wearing masks over their faces jumped out of the open doors of the SUV and roughly pulled and pushed the stunned and hurt Tiwari up from the ground and into the rear of the vehicle.

As Tiwari's gang members began to rush out of the garage premises to check out the reasons for the unexpected commotion, the Tata Safari roared away with its prisoner…

Before the hapless Tiwari could wonder whether his henchmen had the time and opportunity to give chase – something hard smashed into his head and he sank into a bottomless pit of pain and eventual darkness…

The drug lord re-surfaced into consciousness to find himself in a dark room, tightly strapped by the wrists and ankles to a chair. He was unable to move or see anything. His head ached and swam. His chest hurt. He felt sick.

He waited.

After what seemed like a lifetime, he heard the sound of a door opening. There were sounds of movement – and a light bulb was switched on.

The bright yellow glare hit Tiwari like a smash in the face. He reeled back and squeezed his eyes tightly shut. A rough hand grabbed his hair and pulled his head up in a painful grip. Biting back a shout of pain, Tiwari opened his eyes to find himself staring up at a masked face. Only the eyes and lips were visible.

The face hidden behind the black mask now spoke. "Let's keep it short and simple," said Rajat Malhotra. "You cooperate with us – and you won't get hurt..."

In an eventful career involving murder, drug dealing, kidnapping and extortion, spanning over two decades, Tiwari had uttered those very same words many times. Never had these words been addressed to him before. He did not know how to react. He kept quiet.

Rajat Malhotra continued: "Just tell me where I can find Surinder Mishra and your ordeal will be over."

Tiwari did not respond.

Rajat studied his captive for a few seconds and then spoke: "Till eight years ago, before he was jailed, Surinder Mishra was your partner in crime, in your thriving business of kidnapping and extortion. The police caught up with him – but he did not betray you. When he came out of jail, you financed his new venture – the orphanages that acted as a cover for his child trafficking activities. Now that he has bolted, he must have come to you for shelter. Tell me where he is."

Dev Dutt Tiwari just stared at the masked Rajat Malhotra and said nothing.

"Anoop Puri talked before he died in his Kathmandu hotel," lied Rajat. "I have details of your drug dealing collaborations with him in Goa and Manali. You can be put behind bars for the rest of your life if you don't cooperate."

Tiwari maintained his silence. He had clearly decided that this was his safest option in the present circumstances.

A hand that felt as hard as a rock planted a stinging slap across his left cheek with a force that almost turned his head around in a half circle. His neck muscles felt as if they had almost been torn off.

He shut his eyes in pain and humiliation. But he still did not speak.

"The only reason I did not smash your teeth in just now is because I want your mouth intact to tell me where to find Mishra," spat out Rajat. He waited for Tiwari to recover from the slap and open his eyes again.

As the mafia don reopened his eyes, several more light bulbs were switched on. "Look around you," commanded Rajat. He pointed towards the ceiling.

Tiwari looked up – and saw several meat hooks, the kind butchers use to display carcasses, hanging from iron rods crisscrossing the ceiling. A thick wire hung from the curved end of each meat hook.

The drug lord and gang leader looked at the masked Rajat with a puzzled expression on his face.

Rajat was unmerciful. "Right now, my men are camped outside your house in Ghaziabad where your wife and legitimate children reside and also outside your second house in Faridabad where your mistress and bastard children live," he informed a dazed and stunned Tiwari. Rajat raised the cell phone he was holding in his left hand and brought it close to the eyes of the helpless thug strapped to the chair. "One call from me right now and my men will storm both houses and take captive both families. Your guards have already been overpowered – there will be no resistance. The women and children will be brought here – and then hung by their necks from the wires tied to these meat hooks. You will yourself watch your wife, mistress and children die their slow and agonizing deaths – as I'm sure you've watched many of your own captives die before…"

"No!" screamed Tiwari. "Don't do it! I will tell you what I know!"

***

29

Goa

The double-storied shack called Lucia's Hell is located on north Goa's Anjuna beach. It is a flourishing restaurant-bar-hookah joint that is popular with Goa's large and growing expatriate population for several reasons, the foremost being that people openly peddle and consume drugs inside – activities legally banned in Goa. The local police are paid off handsomely by the politically well connected owners and so they turn a blind eye. The shack Lucia's Hell is home to regular rave parties – and loud music is played in its hashish filled atmosphere till very late into the night, all days of the week.

Tonight was no different.

The second floor bar area was dimly lit. The overall colour of the lighting was a dark shade of red. It gave the interiors an eerie and ghostly kind of feel and look that matched the steady thump of trance music pulsating through the heavy duty speakers.

There were foreigners everywhere. Hippies with dreadlocks and backpackers lounged about on plastic chairs or sat sprawled on the floor. Many were taking drags from opium sticks – which were being passed around like toffees at a children's birthday party. The smoke-filled air was laden with intoxicating smells. The crush of bodies and the beat of the rhythmic music made up a mesmerizing ambience.

Two hippies of Indian nationality sat on plastic chairs in a corner of the second floor bar and restaurant of Lucia's Hell shack, and tried to make conversation with the African drug peddler John between low points in the loud music.

"A gram of cocaine will cost you two thousand eight hundred rupees, my friends," said John as he blew smoke rings in the air. "Ten grams of ganja will cost you one thousand rupees. I can also give you an Ecstasy tablet for six hundred rupees."

One of the Indian hippies John was speaking to was Rajat Malhotra. Rajat was completely unrecognizable from his normal handsome self – it is doubtful whether even his father would recognize him as he was now. His thick and very long black matted locks had not been washed for days. His beard was thick and long and very unkempt. Thick lens spectacles covered his eyes.

Rajat's companion, a key member of his Special Operations Unit (SOU), was equally well disguised as a hardcore hippie. The SOU took its undercover operations very seriously.

Rajat was about to respond to the African drug peddler when, suddenly, a bare-chested, heavily tattooed foreign man of seemingly north European origin, sitting at the other end of the large room, screamed in a drug-induced haze. The foreigner's mahogany face was frozen like a waxwork.

Nobody looked in the direction of the screaming foreigner. Rajat tried hard to act similarly nonchalant.

The foreigner lapsed into sullen silence. The music again took over the senses with its overpowering force and rhythmic thumping. The beat was certainly hypnotic, Rajat thought to himself, as he turned his attention back to the African drug peddler.

John wore the glazed look of a hard core heroin addict. His arms were pincushions of needle jabs. Rajat had come to the shack looking for 'doctor' John – the African's regular use of hypodermic syringes had earned him the nickname 'doctor'. John epitomized the drug trade in Goa. He was both consumer and retailer. Proceeds from the sales he made also helped fund his own daily fix. Drugs were also often traded for sexual favours – particularly from the many Russian women who landed in Goa in droves during the winter tourist season, looking to make a fast buck, if not serious money.

It was a Russian that Rajat had come to Goa to track down – the feared leader of the Russian drug mafia that now ruled the Goan underworld. The fear crazed don Dev Dutt Tiwari had given Rajat his name but not the location of his hideout, since the mafia gang leader of western UP did not have any knowledge of this.

But Dev Dutt Tiwari had told Rajat that he had sent Surinder Mishra to hide in Goa under the protection of the Russian mafia – the Russkaya Mafiya – and so it was to Goa that Rajat had come to search out the man who had either murdered his sister or knew who had killed her.

Rajat Malhotra leaned forward and put his lips near John's right ear. "It's not the regular stuff I'm looking for," he said. "I want CK1 pills – lots of them!"

John froze. He stopped blowing smoke rings.

"What are you talking about?" asked John, his face impassive, his tone no longer friendly.

"You know very well what I am talking about, my friend. There is a big demand for CK1 pills in Mumbai – it's the favourite party drug of Mumbai high rollers. There's big money to be made if we can sew up a steady supply. If you help us, there'll be a big cut for you." Rajat leaned back with a satisfied look.

The African gave Rajat a look that was part resentful and part fearful. "I don't know what your game is – but you'd better get out of this shack and off this beach fast. Anjuna beach is the turf of the Israelis. What you're looking for may be available up north – in Morjim beach, where the Russians hang out. If you talk of deal making with the Russians here, in Israeli turf, you could end up with your throat slit. Do us both a favour and get out of here!"

Rajat knew why John was so fearful. Until the year 2003 or

so, British and Israeli gangs controlled Goa's drug trade. Nigerians like John had always been minor players, mainly as couriers with local connections. John had settled down in Goa over a decade ago – and he had depended on the Israeli drug lords from the very beginning, for his livelihood and protection from the police. Since 2004, the Russians had taken over the drug trade in Goa in a big way – and this was severely resented by the Israelis. Gang wars were common. Killings were frequent. The rivalry was bitter.

Israelis were still active and more visible than the Russians, but were slowly but surely getting edged out of the business. Russia was now the narcotics superpower of the world and the Russian mafia – Russkaya Mafia – ruled Goa. The Israelis were not organized enough to face the Russian onslaught, much less overcome it. This made the Israelis extremely sensitive to losing out whatever business and dealers and connections they still had to the Russians.

If the Israelis got to know that their own drug peddler John was talking about doing business in Russian drugs inside their shack on 'their' beach, the African would probably soon find himself inside a sealed iron box at the bottom of the ocean – his body having first been cut into several pieces while the Nigerian was still alive…

And it was, indeed, a Russian manufactured synthetic drug that Rajat had referred to. The Russian mafia in Goa manufactured the heady party drug, the CK1 pill, which had become a craze in Goa and, more importantly, a craze also in India's commercial capital Mumbai, a city which has more party goers than all the countries of Europe put together. The CK1 pill is a combination of cocaine and Ketamine. Sold on the Russian mafia controlled north Goa beaches under the pseudonyms 'Blizzard' and 'Calvin Klein', the demand for CK1 far outstripped supply – and the product was fast acquiring an enviable premium pricing tag.

Rajat had decided that this was the product he would piggyback on, to reach the Russian drug lord Sergei Noborgov – the man who was sheltering Surinder Mishra at the behest of Dev Dutt Tiwari, his north Indian partner in crime. Only talk of a million rupee plus deal could get him to Noborgov personally instead of to a lieutenant. There was only one problem: for reasons of safety, the Russians of Goa guarded their privacy fiercely; they avoided mingling with others and supplied only to their own kind. Outside contacts like Tiwari had been cultivated with a lot of care and out of necessity – this was the only way of reaching Punjab, Manali and Delhi's Paharganj, where the serious money was to be made.

Rajat knew that he would have to use the services of a known drug peddler of Goa – with a decade old track record – to establish initial links with the lieutenants of Sergei Noborgov and thereby to the Russian drug lord himself. His investigations into the activities of the late underworld don he had shot in Kathmandu, Anoop Puri, had given him a name – the Nigerian drug peddler John.

John was also a part time assassin; he needed several sources of income to fund his own daily fix requirements and, like many hardcore drug consumers, was not adverse to indulging in violent crime if that helped raise the necessary monetary resources to feed his addiction.

One such assignment would now come back to haunt him.

Rajat leaned forward again and put his lips close to the African's ear. The trance music blasting out of the speakers spread around the bar-restaurant would drown out his words if he did not speak them clearly and very close to John's ears. Rajat needed John to hear every word he would now utter.

"I appreciate your loyalty to your Israeli masters," Rajat said loudly into the Nigerian's ear. "But does the Israeli drug lord Ben Gurav know that you took money from the mafia lord Anoop Puri to kill his younger brother Yakuv Gurav two years ago?"

***

30

The Russian

The Russian 'invasion' of Goa began about six years ago. Currently, more than ten thousand Russians are settled in Goa. In Morjim, in the extreme north of Goa and in Palolem, in the southern part of Goa, these ten thousand or more Russians live, in small tightly-knit enclaves that have been dubbed 'Little Russia' by the locals.

The ten thousand are just the settlers. Another fifty five thousand or so Russians fly into Goa in eight hundred chartered flights during the tourist season, not just from Moscow but even from small cities like Yekaterinburg and Novosibirsk. Many of the visitors are drug traffickers and drug couriers. Many stay back as either peddlers or users or both.

Sergei Noborgov not only ruled over a gigantic narcotic empire out of his base in Morjim in north Goa, but he also had a vast army of Russians at his command, stationed on Indian soil.

One such henchman, a blond giant with a thick moustache, long hair and tattoos all over his bare chest, now stood next to his parked motorcycle in the middle of the small side road bordering Morjim beach, and pointed the pistol in his hand at John and Rajat. It was the middle of the night. Rajat and John had come to this spot straight from the Lucia's Hell after the Nigerian drug peddler had realized that the Indian hippie he was talking to meant serious business, and had in his possession the information that could turn the African into an instant target for brutal revenge by his Israeli drug lord masters.

"Why did you call me here you boot licker of the Israelis?" snarled the giant Russian, his forefinger tightening around the trigger of the gun in his hand.

John was unfazed. He knew that all this posture was pure drama for the benefit of his companion. The giant Russian called Nevy owed the African a few favours – he would definitely make time to listen. There would be no trigger pulling – at least for the moment.

"I have a big business proposition for Sergei Noborgov," responded John, now back to blowing smoke rings in the air. Even though he wasn't his usual confident self at the moment, appearances still had to be kept.

"Then tell it to Ben Gurav, your lord and master. What are you doing here, in Morjim?"

John wished he knew the answer to that question himself. He looked nervously towards Rajat and said: "This guy here needs a heavy consignment of 'Blizzard'. He needs a steady supply. He says he can pay big money. He has customers in Mumbai."

The giant Russian called Nevy turned his attention to Rajat. His blue eyes surveyed the long haired and thick bearded hippie, standing in front of him, from head to toe. "Sergei Noborgov is not some tight-assed hooker whom *you* can throw money at and then get into bed with," spat Nevy. "Just get lost!"

This is when the other long-haired hippie who had accompanied Rajat to Lucia's Hell sprang into action. This agent of the SOU named Siddhanth Suri, had not accompanied John and Rajat to Morjim to meet Nevy, after the African had spoken to the Russian giant over the phone in front of them. Once it had become clear that the henchman of Sergei Noborgov would meet up with John, to honour past debts, Siddhanth had disappeared. Rajat had not explained this disappearance and John had been too frightened to ask.

The drug peddler John now realized that the second Indian hippie had not disappeared – he had quietly followed the African and Rajat to the meeting point and had stayed hidden from the blonde Russian, until he had been able to position himself strategically right behind him.

Now Siddhanth struck.

Before Nevy could realize what was happening, the barrel of a gun crashed into his head. He crumpled like a deflated balloon with a scream of pain that was cut off by Rajat who quickly sprang forward and clasped his right hand over the falling thug's mouth and caught him by his waist with his left arm to break the fall.

A startled John was stunned by the suddenness of events – but only for a split second. He took to his heels and ran – but was cut down by a bullet that slammed into his left thigh. It was fired from Siddhanth's gun, fitted with an efficient silencer.

John lay on the road, moaning with pain and bleeding. He, however, made no attempt to shout for help – Siddhanth's gun was pointed at his head and the threat was clear. If John shouted, he would invite death.

Rajat, meanwhile, was busy. He had caught the stunned Russian giant by the collar and was planting one punch after the other into his bleeding face. As the blonde Russian slowly slid to the ground under the barrage of punches, his face rapidly turned to a bleeding mess. His lips broke apart into a bloody pulp, his eyes became swollen and red – and his nose cracked.

Eventually, Rajat stopped hitting the Russian and released him. As he surveyed the defeated and bloody giant lying at his feet, Rajat's chest heaved as he recovered his breath after his exertions. Then he addressed the moaning Russian: "You will now take me to Sergei Noborgov, you bastard. Otherwise, I will put a bullet into each of your kneecaps, and then into each eye…"

***

31

More Russians

Cutting through the province of Goa is the Mandovi river – which is as popular a tourist attraction as the numerous golden sand beaches that dot the coast and the warm blue waters of the Arabian Sea, that wash the western border of this blessed part of India, on which nature has chosen to bestow so many favours.

During the peak tourist season, in the winter months, special dusk cruises on the Mandovi – complete with serenading bands – add to the charm of the river.

By midnight, the river empties out and the cruise boats – which are actually large and brightly lit catamarans – retire for the night. There should have been no cruise boat on the Mandovi river at 3 am, which is the quietest part of the night, in any part of the world. But this night, there was one.

The luxury launch was brightly lit and richly decorated. There was a party going on board. The noise was boisterous, the music loud. The mighty river suffered in silence as the launch cruised over the waters, the sounds of merrymaking tearing through the night sky and invading the darkness like mortar shells in a hospital zone. Even the moon, which would normally sparkle in the dark Goan sky, tried to hide its face, behind scattered clouds, in apparent mortification at this ruthless desecration of the night's peace.

The regular sunset and moonlight cruises that are so popular on the Mandovi river treat tourists to traditional Goan dance performances. These cultural performances on the cruise boats make the experience of gliding through the rippling waves even more colourful. The dances that were being performed on this luxury launch at 3 am – long after the regular tourist cruise ships and catamarans had been boarded up for the night – were far from traditional Goan and far from cultural. The dancers were not Goan – they were nubile Russian girls. And the dancers were not dressed in traditional Goan dresses – in fact the Russian girls who were dancing away in drug fuelled frenzy were not dressed in anything much at all...

The Russian drug lord who ruled the Goan underworld and who was now entertaining key foreign and Indian suppliers and clients on this luxury launch, himself lolled on a deckchair on the main deck with a bikini clad blonde girl on each side of him. The three shared a lit joint stick and limitless shots of vodka. The live band rocked the night as Sergei Noborgov and his blondes alternately took drags on the hashish stick they were sharing and swigs from the vodka bottles. All around them, leading drug dealers of the world, guests of the Russian drug lord, similarly entertained themselves with girls, dope and booze.

The luxury launch approached the Mandovi Bridge, which majestically spans the Mandovi river, linking the towns of Panjim and Porvorim.

The darkness below the Mandovi Bridge kept hidden from those partying on the luxury launch, even if the merry makers were inclined to survey the river view which they were most certainly not, three police launches parked there in the deep waters. These police launches were filled with Goan police personnel and members of the Special Operations Unit of the Indian Home Ministry. Everyone on board the three police launches was armed to the teeth.

The blonde Russian giant called Nevy had talked – though with some difficulty, since his mouth had been smashed to a pulp. Rajat was informed where to find the Russian drug lord Sergei Noborgov. He had contacted his seniors in the Home Ministry – some were woken up from sleep by his unexpected call in the middle of the night – and had got urgent instructions sent to the top Goan police authorities to give full support and cooperation to the SOU operatives who were working on 'Operation Blizzard', which was the name given to his mission of smashing the Russian drug mafia in Goa.

Speed was imperative – lest the many corrupt Goan police personnel in the pay of the Russian drug lords got wind of the plans to raid the luxury launch of Sergei Noborgov and alert him…

As the launch and its load of merrymakers neared the Mandovi Bridge, the three police launches revved into action…

The raid was short and swift. The pleasure seekers on board were in no condition to stand on two feet – much less put up a resistance to the armed policemen and commandoes who suddenly sprang out of nowhere and boarded the ship. The bodyguards of the world's top drug dealers were as doped out as their masters and were easily disarmed and made captive. The drug lords suffered the same fate. Noborgov was completely smashed and watched the proceedings in a drug induced haze, his right wrist handcuffed to the left wrist of one of his bikini clad blonde girlfriends.

Rajat Malhotra had carried with him a photograph of his prey. He found Surinder Mishra in a cabin below the deck lying doped out on a bunk, his eyes glazed from too much drug taking, his cheeks pale and sunken. But he was alive. He would be made to talk…

***

32

Plot Twists

The emergency meeting took place in the office room of Commissioner of Gurgaon Police, Rajender Saxena.

"Surinder Mishra says he did not kill Anamika," announced Detective Superintendent Avinash Sharma. "This matches what Aggarwal also told us before he was killed. But Surinder Mishra did go to the Malhotra house that night to kill her."

"Then what happened?" asked Rajender Saxena.

"He bumped into Sudesh Aggarwal in the rear garden of the house – just after he had climbed over the wall," responded Avinash.

"They were not working together?" asked the Police Commissioner, surprised.

"No. Mishra's decision to kill Anamika was his alone. He panicked when he discovered that she was making enquiries about his background. He got upset when he came to know that she had tried to speak to some of the runaway children to find out what was bothering them and where they had come from in the first place," contributed Detective Inspector Ramesh Uppal. "Surinder Mishra was afraid that, if Anamika was not stopped quickly, the whole child trafficking racket behind Save the Children in Distress would blow up in his face and he would land back in jail. This he intended to avoid at all costs."

"So he decided to kill Anamika," said Avinash, "but did not consult his co-partners in crime – Rama Prasad Aggarwal, Sudesh Aggarwal and Rani Suri. He thought that they would not agree to such a drastic solution to this potential problem."

"And he was wrong?" queried Rajender Saxena.

"He realized he was wrong in this assumption when he met up with a masked Sudesh Aggarwal in the garden of the Malhotra house on that fateful night," concluded Avinash.

"From all that Mishra told us during his interrogation, it appears that the encounter in the garden was quite a dramatic one," observed Ramesh.

"I can imagine…" commented Rajender Saxena.

"Both accused each other of hiding their plans to commit murder – which was true – and almost came to blows," continued Ramesh.

"I wonder how the guards of the Malhotra house missed all this?" questioned Rajender Saxena. The Commissioner of Gurgaon Police and his two junior officers instinctively turned their eyes to the fourth occupant of the room, Rajat Malhotra.

Rajat looked grim. "The guards were either paid to turn a blind eye or were sleeping on the job," he observed. "If it's the former, then we may get a lead from them to the identity of the person who bribed them – whether it was Surinder Mishra, Sudesh Aggarwal or a third party." Rajat looked at Avinash. "I think the guards should be picked up for questioning."

"I agree with you," responded Avinash, who, along with Rajender Saxena and Ramesh Uppal was now very aware of Rajat Malhotra's secret life as a special agent of the Indian Intelligence Service. He spoke into his cellphone and gave the necessary instructions. "Of course, the guards present at the house that night were subjected to routine questioning about what they had or had not seen that night," continued Avinash, "but they were not treated as suspects. Now, we will investigate the angle of connivance…."

"Was the house security outsourced?" asked Rajender Saxena.

"Yes, to the same security agency that provides guards to all the establishments of Malhotra Industries – offices, factories and godowns."

"I would suggest that you conduct a background check on the security agency that supplied the guards," suggested Rajender Saxena to Avinash. "The guards may not have been bribed directly by the people who planned the murder – but may have been instructed to slacken security that night by their superiors in the security agency."

"Quite possible. We will of course, get to the truth when we interrogate the guards – but we should also do a scan of the security agency," agreed Avinash. He spoke into his cellphone again.

"Let's now return to Surinder Mishra's confession," said Rajat. "Is he claiming that Sudesh Aggarwal killed my sister?"

"Yes," responded Avinash Sharma. "He claims that Sudesh Aggarwal asked him to wait near the rear wall and keep a watch out for the guards, while he entered the house and completed the job he had come for…"

"Which was to kill my sister!" observed Rajat grimly.

"Yes, but which sister…?" commented Avinash slowly.

Rajender Saxena, Ramesh Uppal and Rajat Malhotra stared at Avinash Sharma. "What are you saying?" asked Rajat. "What do you mean by saying which sister?"

"After you pointed out that the police had missed out the Director of Fundraising of Save the Children in Distress Society from the investigations, I immediately ordered a background check and a report on recent movements and activities of Sudesh Aggarwal," responded Avinash. "The report on his recent movements and activities was very interesting. He had been spotted at many places Aradhana Malhotra was also seen at – the same restaurants, showrooms and events. It appears that Sudesh Aggarwal, the son of Rama Prasad Aggarwal, had not only befriended Anamika Malhotra and brought her into the Society – but he had also been stalking her sister Aradhana Malhotra…

***

33

New Revelations

"Why should anybody want to stalk Aradhana?" exclaimed a completely baffled Rajat. "She may have been Anamika's twin, but the sisters did not look identical. It could not have been a case of mistaken identity!"

"There could be a reason – but that would mean that Sudesh Aggarwal had a connection with mysterious activities in one of your father's companies, in addition to his criminal activities linked to the Society…" informed Avinash.

"What!"

As Commissioner of Gurgaon Police Rajender Saxena and Ramesh Uppal looked on, Avinash briefed Rajat about the revelations that had been made by his sister Aradhana, during the initial days of the investigation, regarding the separate death threats received by both Anamika and her, and the investigations the two girls had commenced in their separate workplaces.

"So that is why you started investigating the activities of the Society!" exclaimed Rajat. "Anamika's suspicions were correct – she was actually working for a gang of criminals. Her death has led to the busting of their operations and the death and capture of two of the criminals. But what about Aradhana's suspicions regarding activities at her place of work? Have you made any investigations in that direction?"

"I'm afraid not," admitted Avinash. "The unraveling of the criminal activities of Anamika's employer has taken place so rapidly and the subsequent events like Aggarwal's murder and Mishra's capture have been so stunning that we have not had the time to apply our minds to the other lead. But now, with this new angle of Sudesh Aggarwal's interest in Aradhana's movements, it seems that there is a deeper story and deeper plot behind Anamika's death. Surinder Mishra's confession has thrown new light on the events of the night of the murder. If he did not carry out his plan to kill Anamika, but made way for Sudesh Aggarwal, then who was the intended victim of the man who finally committed the deadly act? I can only make a wild guess – was the real target of the killer Aradhana and not Anamika?"

"We first need to find out just what are these suspicious activities that are taking place in my father's company – and what is Sudesh Aggarwal's connection, if any, with them." Rajat looked stonily at Avinash. "Does my father know of Aradhana's suspicions?"

"When your sister made her revelation to me, she told me that she had not informed either your father or you of her suspicions," responded Avinash. "She was very afraid that she would discover a connection with Devesh Malhotra himself." Avinash locked eyes with the scion of the Malhotra dynasty when he uttered these words.

Rajat turned red in the face. "I hope you understand that you are referring to one of the most respected men in India today, Superintendent!"

Avinash saw no reason to lock horns with Rajat. "I am aware of your father's standing in society and of his achievements. I am only informing you that your sister was not confident to share her suspicions with her father…"

Rajat kept quiet. Rajender Saxena intervened. "I think that a meeting with Aradhana is required immediately; not only must we know what she had discovered at her place of work to warrant a death threat, we must also provide her with police protection. If she was a target earlier – she still remains in danger, particularly since Sudesh Aggarwal is still at large."

Rajat was quick to react to this. "Why should Sudesh Aggarwal still be at large? I smashed the top mafia gang of western UP and captured the drug and underworld king of Goa so that we could lay hands on Surinder Mishra, who would lead us to the real killer, if Surinder himself was not the one who had murdered Anamika. So why don't we extract from Surinder Mishra where Sudesh Aggarwal is hiding?"

"We have some leads – but not the complete details," informed Ramesh. "Sudesh Aggarwal disappeared immediately after Anamika's death. That's why he was never around when we visited the offices of Save the Children in Distress Society. When we told Rama Prasad Aggarwal of Anamika's death, he was shocked, since he had no knowledge of any such plan, and he later summoned and questioned Surinder Mishra – who told him about the events in the Malhotra grounds that night."

"The news that his son had, in all probability, committed a murder, completely shattered Rama Prasad Aggarwal – and led him into a confessional mode," said Avinash. "He wanted to protect himself from a probable murder charge – and expose his son."

"So it was Sudesh Aggarwal who killed his own father?" asked Rajat.

"That is the other shocker that has come from Mishra's confession," responded Avinash. "Mishra was very much present in the Gurgaon orphanage that day when Aggarwal spoke to me over the phone, when I was on my way to the Panipat orphanage. He saw who killed Aggarwal in order to prevent him from uttering the name of Anamika's murderer."

"Aggarwal's killer was Rani Suri," contributed Ramesh.

***

34

A Daughter's Suspicions

Aradhana Malhotra sat at her desk in her office, in the administration block of Malhotra Computer Products Limited, and studied the evidence. She could not make head or tail of the documents she was reading.

Aradhana worked in the Marketing Department. This was her area of specialization – this is what she had focused her studies on during her Masters in Business Administration. Purchase was not her forte. Yet purchase and procurement documents are what she was studying this evening, in the quiet after office hours, when the building was empty of all employees but for the security personnel, guarding the entrances to the administration building and to the factory complex.

Aradhana had enough commercial savvy to understand the contents of the invoice copies and other purchase related documents, which she had clandestinely obtained from the factory complex behind her office; she had obtained these documents from a junior purchase officer through a mixture of bribery and pulling of weight, as the daughter of the Chairman and Managing Director of the company. What Aradhana could not understand was the arithmetic. The figures did not add up.

For several months, the Marketing team of Malhotra Computer Products Limited (owner of the MCPL brand), of which Aradhana was a senior member, had faced a unique problem. Faced with ambitious sales targets – and a looming year closing – the Marketing team had employed out of the box strategies and aggressive selling techniques to try and maximize bulk orders from corporate clients for MCPL personal computers and laptops and peripherals like laser jet printers. They were very successful in this – and looked forward to bumper year end sales. There was only one serious obstacle in their path. And it was a problem not caused by competitors but raised by their own organization.

The bumper orders had been procured by packaging of computers and printers as one composite product unit and offering discounts on such 'combined unit' purchases in bulk by corporate clients. The orders had poured in – but deliveries had become a major issue.

There were computers, in plenty, lying in stock with the company – but no printers. Nobody in the department seemed to have an explanation for this…

The purchase related documents that had been clandestinely obtained by Aradhana told a completely opposite story, at least to her untrained eye. The purchase of the various machine parts that were required for assembling of laser jet printers were actually double of the procurement of parts required for assembly of personal computers. This anomaly had been going on for several months now. There should not have been any shortage of printers – in fact, the stock of printers should have far exceeded the stock of personal computers in the storage godowns of the company.

So, why had the printers not been assembled? Or, if they had been assembled, then where were they stored? Why were they not available for sale?

Aradhana felt the familiar dull ache return to her head as these thoughts flashed across her mind. All was not right at Malhotra Computer Products Limited. There were several unresolved and mysterious issues that she had come across, like unscheduled and late night production runs and strange, late night truck movements. She did not know who to share this information with, without compromising her father.

She was a daughter caught in a conflict between parental loyalty and exposing wrongful activity. What if her father, the highly respected Devesh Malhotra, was involved in some wrong doing?

For wrong doing was definitely at the bottom of several strange observations that Aradhana had made during her employment with the company – of this she was now convinced....

Aradhana again pondered over why she was reluctant to confide her doubts even to her elder brother Rajat. Her brother also had secrets – and this had made Aradhana extremely uneasy about Rajat's bonafides. He owned an import and export business, to whose offices she had never been invited. Rajat was frequently travelling – where to had never been discussed or revealed. He was often not contactable over phone or e-mail – and no explanations had ever been given for this.

No, it would be difficult for Aradhana to confide in her brother. An uneasy thought flashed through her mind – not for the first time; what if her father and brother were together involved in some illegal or unethical activity?

Aradhana shook herself vigorously and jumped to her feet. She could not brood like this much longer – she would go mad. She needed to clear her head. And she desperately needed to dig deeper into the mysterious goings on in the company…

***

35

Security

The three security guards, who had been standing guard at the gates of the Malhotra Mansion on the night of Anamika's murder, were no longer traceable. They had vanished. An extremely angry Detective Superintendent Avinash Sharma confronted the General Manager of Allied Security & Protection Services, in the latter's office in Gurgaon's Cyber City office complex. It was evening, but Avinash had telephoned ahead of coming and had asked the senior most official of the Gurgaon branch to wait for him.

The GM of the security agency was a retired Colonel. He looked extremely uncomfortable under the angry glare of Avinash.

"I assure you, Superintendent, that I had no knowledge that the three guards were no longer reporting for duty," said Colonel Onkar Nath. "I only discovered this now when you asked to meet them."

A biting comment regarding the efficiency of this retired

Colonel sprang to Avinash's lips, but he bit back the words. Instead, he said: "Somebody in your organization must have known that the three guards were missing – that they had not reported for duty and are still not available!"

"Of-of course! Their immediate supervisor was Captain Rastogi. He is the one who has just informed me over the phone that the guards have not been reporting for duty after their police questioning."

"I would like to meet him, please – right now!"

"Captain Rastogi is not here right now, Superintendent. He has gone over to the office and factory complex of Malhotra Computer Products Limited in Udyog Vihar. We provide guards to all the establishments of Malhotra Industries – offices and factories and godowns, as well as the residences of the owners."

Avinash glanced at his watch. "It's after office hours now – what work would Captain Rastogi have there?" he asked.

"I wouldn't know – our supervisors have a free hand to carry out their responsibilities."

Avinash glanced at Ramesh and a sudden suspicion flashed through his mind. "Which of her father's companies does Aradhana work for?" he asked his junior colleague.

"Malhotra Computer Products Limited," responded Detective Inspector Ramesh Uppal.

The penny dropped. Avinash swung around to face the Colonel. He held out his hand. "Please give me your cell phone," he ordered.

The Colonel made as if to protest, but then shrugged his shoulders. He picked up his cell phone from his desk and handed it over to Avinash. "You seem to be harbouring some suspicions about me, Superintendent," said Colonel Onkar Nath, his face cold. "Whatever they are – they are wrong."

"We'll see. Right now Colonel, you will kindly accompany us. I want to make sure that you do not contact Captain Rastogi under any circumstances." So saying, Avinash turned and strode out of the room.

Ramesh looked at the Colonel. With a blank look, Colonel Onkar Nath followed Avinash out of his office room – closely followed by Ramesh.

The drive to the office and factory complex of MCPL in Gurgaon's Udyog Vihar was short and swift. During the drive in the police jeep, which was closely followed by another jeep carrying armed policemen, a call was quickly made to Rajat Malhotra. "Any idea where your sister is?" asked Avinash.

Rajat was quick to respond. "I'm waiting for her at home. She's still at the MCPL office."

A cold hand clutched the heart of Avinash. "Shit!" he exclaimed in uncharacteristic fashion. "I think your sister's in grave danger!"

***

36

A Girl in Danger

Aradhana decided that she had done enough investigative work for the day. She had no need now to study the purchase department papers any further. The figures were clear – it was their interpretation that was puzzling. Purchases of small parts required for assembling printers far exceeded the number and quantity of parts procured for the making of computers – yet printers were in short supply, computers were not. This was just one of the several mysterious and puzzling things that Aradhana had stumbled upon, during her employment in her father's company. Now she needed to decide what she would do with the information and observations she had gathered. Who would she confide in?

A thought flashed into her mind. Could she confide in Detective Superintendent Avinash Sharma? The police officer was investigating her sister's murder – Aradhana's observations might not help him in that matter, but the detective could help solve the MCPL mysteries....

Aradhana froze. The threat! She had almost forgotten about the threat to her life – the advice to mind her own business! That threat had been conveyed to Anamika over the telephone, but the caller had uttered the name Aradhana repeatedly. Had the threat been made to the wrong person? Was Aradhana the real target?

The mysterious activities at MCPL were piling up – Aradhana would have to take a call fast on what to do with her observations. Should she confide in the police officer or her father or her brother?

Aradhana looked down at the papers lying on her table and realized that she had another more urgent priority. She would need to return the purchase department papers from where she had picked them up – otherwise the culprits, if there were any culprits, would be alerted that somebody had discovered their secret.

As Aradhana gathered up the invoice copies and stock statements, which she had promised the junior purchase officer (who had given them to her) she would return to the relevant purchase department filing cabinets this day itself, this daughter of Devesh Malhotra had another sad thought: was it her father or her brother who had been behind that death threat?

Aradhana stepped out of her office knowing full well that she continued to be in a state of dilemma: she could not confide to the police without compromising her father and, perhaps, her brother....

Aradhana shrugged off these thoughts and concentrated on the more immediate and pressing matter of returning the documents to the purchase department. She strode down the quiet corridors of the MCPL administrative block, conscious of the brooding silence that had enveloped the building after all the employees had left. She knew that there were security guards patrolling the building but doubted that there was anybody else around, except her.

It was just after Aradhana had replaced the folders that she realized that she had been wrong – she was not the only official who was still present in the complex.

As Aradhana stepped out of the lift that had taken her down to the ground floor cafeteria area, she came face to face with her father.

***

37

The Woman With No Past

While Detective Superintendent Avinash Sharma and Detective Inspector Ramesh Uppal were racing to the company's headquarters in Gurgaon, to prevent what they thought was the possibility of grievous harm to Aradhana Malhotra, their chief, Commissioner Rajender Saxena, also rushed to another destination – the government owned and run Gurgaon Civil Hospital. The prisoner Surinder Mishra had been brought to the hospital from the Gurgaon jail, where he had been lodged, in a serious condition. The former Director Programmes of Save the Children in Distress Society had been badly beaten up by fellow prison inmates.

The severely injured prisoner had specifically asked to speak directly to the topmost official of the Gurgaon police force before lapsing into unconsciousness. The doctors attending to Surinder

Mishra had informed the Police Commissioner's office that the injured prisoner had several internal injuries, as a result of the beating he had received – and that his chances of surviving the surgery were fifty per cent either way. Hence, Rajender Saxena had rushed to Mishra's bedside, before he was wheeled in for surgery and before his lieutenants Avinash Sharma and Ramesh Uppal could join him.

When Rajender Saxena stepped past the saluting police guards outside the door and entered the hospital room, he saw Mishra lying, hooked to a saline drip and connected through various tubes to several machines designed to prolong life. He hoped that the injured prisoner would be in a condition to talk. He need not have worried. The police commissioner was relieved to see that the heavily bandaged Surinder Mishra had recovered consciousness enough to recognize that a very senior police official was standing next to his bed. The prisoner managed to raise his hand in a kind of half salute.

Rajender Saxena sat down on a chair, that had been quickly drawn up to the side of the bed by his police aide. Under the watchful eyes of the nurse on duty, he lowered he head until his lips were close to Surinder Mishra's ears and whispered: "You wanted to speak to me?"

For a minute or so, Mishra said nothing. Rajender Saxena noted that the prisoner's eyes were bloody and swollen – they must have been at the receiving end of several powerful punches. The man's lips were likewise swollen and split. The nose was in equally bad shape – broken out of shape and bandaged. The rest of the face and head were also bandaged. He could not see the body from neck down, as it was covered with a thick hospital sheet, but he knew that most of it was also broken and thoroughly bandaged.

The internal damage must have been considerable. Mishra was clearly using almost superhuman determination to keep himself conscious enough to try and talk.

"The prisoners were instigated to beat me to death," suddenly whispered Surinder Mishra. "They were paid..."

Rajender Saxena stiffened. He waited for Surinder to continue.

The prisoner did not continue immediately. He lay on the bed, his eyes closed. Saxena waited patiently.

"Rani Suri paid them to kill me..." he whispered – and again lapsed into silence.

By now, a doctor had entered the room. "Sir, I suggest that we let the patient rest a bit before we take him to the operation theatre."

Rajender Saxena ignored the doctor. Surinder Mishra was clearly in great pain, but had not finished with talking – of this the police commissioner was very sure.

His patience was rewarded. Mishra, with great effort, opened his lips again and spoke softly, his eyes still shut: "Rani Suri is a terrorist plant..." Rajender Saxena froze. The doctor made as if to speak again, but the police commissioner waved him down with an imperious jerk of his arm. With every nerve in his body tingling, he put his mouth close to Mishra's bandaged ear and asked: "Which terrorist group are you referring to?"

"Al Qaeda..." the words came out in a whisper – but hit Rajender Saxena like a sledgehammer.

Mishra lapsed back into silence, eyes tightly shut and face deathly pale, clearly drained out completely by the effort of speaking. The doctor and the nurse looked worried, but said nothing to the police commissioner. Though they could not hear what was being spoken, it was clear to everyone in the room that the prisoner was making some kind of confession. The Commissioner looked completely riveted.

Rajender Saxena was, in fact, more than riveted. He knew that some explosive revelations were being made by the injured man. But how much of it was true? Could the criminal be believed?

As if reading his mind, Mishra half opened his eyes and, with great effort, resumed his painful attempt to talk. He whispered: "I will be silenced because I know too much. I was paid to bring Rani Suri into Save the Children in Distress Society. She is a member of Al-Qaeda. I helped create her forged documents. Sudesh Aggarwal had gambling and drug purchase related debts – he would have been killed by the mafia. He too was bought over by the terrorists..." the words faded away.

There was a tense silence in the hospital room. Everybody was quiet – the police commissioner, the policeman aide to the commissioner, the doctor, the nurse and Mishra. Rajender Saxena dared not disturb the injured prisoner or pressurize him to speak. He waited for the him to gather the strength to continue.

The lips opened again, though his eyes remained shut. He made an effort to speak – and the police commissioner leaned forward.

"Rani Suri prompted Sudesh Aggarwal to kill Aradhana Malhotra," When – when I bumped into Sudesh in the Malhotra's garden, he – he pretended that he had come there to kill Anamika. But his real target was Aradhana…" the words faded away again.

A very worried Rajender Saxena threw caution to the winds. He knew that this confession needed to be completed. Mishra was revealing all because he wanted to get even with those who had paid to have him beaten to death. But would he live long enough to complete his story? The Commissioner again put his lips very close to Mishra's ear and asked, as clearly and as loudly as he dared: "Where are Rani Suri and Sudesh Aggarwal to be found? What is the target of the terrorists? What are their plans?"

Mishra said nothing. He lay on the hospital bed with his eyes shut. He looked like death. The doctor stepped forward but was stopped by Saxena's raised hand. They both stared at the dying prisoner as he suddenly opened his eyes and made one last herculean effort to share his secrets.

"The terrorists are camped in Bhiwadi," whispered Surinder Mishra through his broken lips. "In the ashram of the nuns…" The breathing became heavy and the next few words came out in a gasp. "The others work in the factory," and his voice trailed off.

***

38

Sense of Danger

Devesh Malhotra was standing in the centre of the cafeteria of the administrative block of Malhotra Computer Products Limited with a perplexed look on his face. The bewildered expression turned to one of shock when he saw his daughter walk in.

"What are you doing here at this time?"

Aradhana was herself in a state of shock, at so suddenly and unexpectedly seeing her father. She turned pale and said nothing.

Devesh Malhotra stared at Aradhana and a worried look replaced the bewildered expression on his face. "He called you here also, did he?" Devesh asked his daughter.

Aradhana wondered whether she had heard right. "What?"

His face turned grim. "Is this some kind of a trick?" he asked with an edge in his voice.

It was her turn to look bewildered. "What are you saying?

Just what is going on?"

"You are not here because of the phone call?"

"What phone call, papa?"

Devesh looked around him and sat down on the nearest chair. He indicated to Aradhana to sit down. Aradhana's legs were beginning to feel like jelly, and she gladly complied.

Father and daughter sat in silence for a minute or so, observing each other. Then Devesh Malhotra spoke: "Somebody telephoned me an hour back – to come here quickly to meet a person who would throw light on Anamika's murder. He told me that Anamika's killing had nothing to do with Save the Children in Distress Society – that the police were following a wrong lead. I would get to learn the truth if I came here quickly. So here I am. And you?"

Aradhana decided to ignore the query for the moment. She quickly put in a counter question: "Who was the person who called you, papa?"

"Don't know." Devesh looked grim. "It was a man's voice – but I did not recognize it, nor the phone number. The caller did not give his name. He cut the connection after conveying his message. I did not call the police or anybody else or try to get the number checked. I just rushed here so as not to miss this person."

Aradhana looked very thoughtful. "There's nobody on the premises, papa," she said, "other than the security personnel…"

Devesh looked puzzled. "Are you sure?" He frowned and continued: "If this is a trick – then what's the purpose of it?"

Aradhana's cellphone buzzed. It was Rajat. She listened to her brother in stunned silence and then said: "I've not been approached by any security guard, not by any of their supervisors. In fact, I'm sitting in the cafeteria with papa. He's come here as a result of some prank phone call." She listened with growing trepidation to her brother's next words and then cut the connection. Aradhana stared at her father with concern written all over her face.

Devesh Malhotra saw the look of worry on Aradhana's face and quickly got up from his chair and strode over to his daughter. He put an arm around her shoulders. "What's the matter, dear? Why are you looking so shocked. Whom were you talking to?"

"It was Rajat, papa. He's on his way here – very near the gates. The police are also on the way. They fear that I'm in danger – that there will be an attempt on my life!"

"What – who?!?"

Aradhana jumped to her feet. "They think that some of the guards from the security agency could be plotting to harm me. Maybe they're after you too – that's why you've been lured here by that mysterious phone call!"

Devesh Malhotra's face became resolute. "Then let's get away from here, fast!"

"That's what Rajat suggested, too. He's advised us to rush to our cars – and to stop for no one. He'll try and meet us in the parking area..."

Father and daughter looked at each other in a moment of

bonding, brought about by mutual love and shared danger. Devesh then grabbed Aradhana's hand and headed for the door. "Is there something going on here that I'm not aware of, Aradhana?" he asked, while pushing open the cafeteria doors and striding into the lobby.

Aradhana felt a great weight lift from her shoulders as she said: "Yes, papa, there is something mysterious going on in MCPL that needs investigating…"

Father and daughter were outside the building by now. The sun was setting and a soft darkness was beginning to envelope the building compound. There were only two cars in the parking lot – Devesh Malhotra's black Mercedes and Aradhana's white Hyundai Accent.

They came to a halt in the middle of the parking area and stared in amazement at the towering gates of the MCPL headquarters. The gates were wide open. There were no security guards in sight.

Devesh looked around puzzled. "Where's my driver?"

An icy wind chilled Aradhana's veins. She tried not to let the fear engulf her. "This does not look good," she said softly.

Devesh held her hand tightly. "No, it does not look good – but don't panic. Let's get out of here in your car. Let's not waste time looking for my driver!"

Father and daughter turned towards Aradhana's car. As they stepped forward, a Pajero raced through the open gates of the complex and screeched to a halt in front of them. Rajat jumped out from the driver's side, his face unusually worked up.

"Is everything OK? Where are the guards? Why are the gates open?"

"The guards are missing. They've left the gates open. My driver's missing," informed Devesh Malhotra quickly.

The two police jeeps carrying Detective Superintendent Avinash Sharma, Detective inspector Ramesh Uppal and the police bodyguards had also arrived on the scene by now. Avinash and Ramesh joined the three members of the Malhotra family – and heard Devesh Malhotra's words.

Avinash looked around him. "I smell a set-up," he observed. He looked at Colonel Onkar Nath whom he had compelled to accompany them. "Your security guards are missing – your security supervisor Captain Rastogi is nowhere to be seen. I don't know how involved you are in all this funny business – but things don't look good for you or your security agency!"

The Colonel was shaken. He clearly realized that his organization had been compromised. He said: "I don't know what is going on, Superintendent, but, for what it's worth, here is a tip – Captain Rastogi is a well known bomb expert. He was an explosives specialist in the Indian army before he took early retirement and joined us."

Rajat Malhotra immediately stiffened. "Of course!" he exclaimed. "Now I understand why there's nobody around – why the guards and the driver have disappeared!"

Devesh and Aradhana looked at Rajat puzzled, but not Avinash and Ramesh. The police officers realized that Rajat's mind, sharpened by commando training, had managed to piece together the strange circumstances and Colonel Nath's information into a definitive clue…

Rajat ran towards Aradhana's car. As the others watched in silence, he lowered himself into a crouch and stared at the lower body of the white Hyundai Accent. He sat for several seconds. A tiny light flickered momentarily from the underbelly of the car. Only because Rajat had fixed his gaze – and only because he had known what to look for – he had noticed the momentary flicker of light.

With a look on his face that was a mixture of anger, horror and shock, Rajat got to his feet and walked over to his father's Mercedes. When he was a few feet away from the car, he crouched on the ground and repeated his staring act. He was not disappointed. A light flickered momentarily below the Mercedes and then vanished.

Satisfied that he was not mistaken in his findings, a grim looking Rajat Malhotra quickly got to his feet and strode over to where his father, sister and the police officers.

"Please call your bomb disposal squad here quickly," he told Avinash. "Two bombs are fixed below the cars of my father and sister. I suspect that each bomb is programmed to go off as soon as the key is inserted into the ignition and turned…"

***

39

The Killers

"Surinder Mishra is dead – and we need to move fast!" announced Commissioner Rajender Saxena. "We now know who killed Anamika. It was Sudesh Aggarwal. But his actual target was Aradhana. We now know that there is a terrorist angle to the whole mystery. We can safely conclude that the 'factory' that Surinder Mishra was referring to, in his dying statement to me, was the MCPL complex. Some terrorists have infiltrated MCPL as factory workers. We have no idea what conspiracy they are planning – but Aradhana has uncovered some pointers which we need to follow through and decipher. Several employees of Allied Security & Protection Services are also involved in the terrorist conspiracy – that much is clear. We need to track them down – particularly Captain Rastogi, the bomb expert. Colonel Nath seems to be above board. This woman named Rani Suri also appears to be a leading member of the terrorists – we now have an indication, given by Surinder Mishra, that she may be holed up in an ashram of nuns in Bhiwadi…" He looked towards Avinash. "This ashram should not be difficult to track down, I assume?"

"It's already on my radar, sir!" responded Avinash. "The place is called Centre of Knowledge and Positive Change. It comprises of a twenty acre campus on the outskirts of Bhiwadi, which, as you know, is an industrial township located on the Rajasthan and Haryana border. It's about an hour's drive from Gurgaon – we will have to cross into Rajasthan. The place is run by a spiritual society of nuns, but there are also male monks amongst the members. The campus contains an auditorium, a hostel and offices and classrooms. There are many visitors to this place. They come for training and meditation. Many of the visitors are foreigners."

"According to what Mishra told me on his death bed, we can assume that Rani Suri and Sudesh Aggarwal and other terrorists can be found hiding in this so-called Centre of Knowledge," commented Rajender Saxena. "But we cannot just barge in there and conduct a raid on a hypothesis. We'll need to move fast but systematically. First of all, put a twenty four hour watch over the campus. Put plainclothesmen on the job – as many as you can, all around the complex. They may discover something incriminating. Let's also check the backgrounds of the foreign visitors – let's go back a year or so. Put our research teams on the job. And Avinash and Ramesh you could pay a courtesy visit…."

"This was already on my mind, sir," responded Avinash Sharma.

"I would not recommend an official visit at this stage," interjected Rajat Malhotra.

All eyes turned to Rajat. His father Devesh and sister Aradhana, who were present at this meeting in the office of the Gurgaon Police Commissioner, had still not got over the shock of discovering his secret life as an undercover intelligence operative of the Indian government. They had many questions to ask – but events were moving too fast to give them an opportunity to confront him with their queries. Rajender Saxena was irritated at this interruption from Rajat and showed it but not Avinash, who had come to respect this man's judgement and capabilities.

"Why don't you think Ramesh and I should pay a visit to the Centre of Knowledge?" Avinash asked Rajat.

"Because this will alert any terrorists or anti-social elements hiding there," responded Rajat. "Rani Suri and Sudesh Aggarwal and possibly other members of the terrorist plot that Mishra referred to, in his dying statement, will not know about his revelations to Commissioner saab. It is in our interest not to alert them, that we know more than they think we know..."

Avinash looked at Rajender Saxena and said: "I think he is right about this, sir! We should mount our surveillance of the complex in Bhiwadi but not alert the people there by openly exposing our suspicions with a police visit."

Rajender Saxena conceded this. "All right! But quickly put our plainclothes surveillance teams in place and start the background checks on recent visitors. Whatever dastardly plot is being hatched there may have progressed to a near complete stage. We shouldn't be caught napping."

Devesh Malhotra had been listening attentively to this exchange of words and he now turned to Aradhana.

"It appears that the terrorist plot has a connection with one of my factories. Can you throw some light on what discoveries you have made at MCPL, Aradhana?"

Aradhana nodded. She no longer doubted her father. Both her father and she had been the target of car bombs earlier that evening. Her father had been lured to the MCPL factory by a mysterious phone call so that a bomb could be planted in his car – that much was obvious. The security guards and their supervisor, Captain Rastogi, as well as Devesh Malhotra's driver, were all missing and the police had sounded an alert for them. The SIM card which had been used to make the phone call to Devesh had been taken in a false name, using false documentation – this much the police had gathered through quick investigation.

Aradhana Malhotra no longer doubted her father or brother. A great load had been lifted from her shoulders. She was eager to reveal her discoveries and suspicions. She poured out her observations of mysterious activities at the factory complex-unscheduled and late night production runs and strange late night truck movements and excessive purchase of printer parts…

At the end of Aradhana's narration there was a confused silence.

"Missing laser printers?" asked Rajender Saxena. "How would this tie up with a terrorist plot?"

***

40

Funny Business in Bhiwadi

A million stars were out. The night was clear and chilly. The police surveillance teams were in place when the gates of the Centre of Knowledge in Bhiwadi swung open and three Maruti Eeco vans raced out of the complex.

The police teams on watch duty went into a flurry of activity. There was a scramble to board the hidden police jeeps. The drivers quickly brought to life the engines of their respective vehicles. Mobile phone handsets were pulled out of jacket pockets and rapid co-ordination was done through hastily barked instructions, to ensure that none of the vans was allowed to disappear without a police tail.

The Centre of Knowledge complex in Bhiwadi had been completely surrounded by police teams that had been sent out from Gurgaon by Avinash Sharma. There were enough jeeps and armed policemen positioned around the complex to ensure that all the three Maruti vans, that had unexpectedly emerged from the gates in the middle of the night, were carefully followed – but at a discreet distance.

The vans had separate destinations. They were tailed by separate police teams. They all made very short trips – to separate factories in Bhiwadi.

Avinash had just hit the bed when the phone call from Bhiwadi pulled him awake. What he heard over the phone washed away all remnants of sleep. As the stream of reports from the police teams following the vans filtered in, Avinash, who lived alone in blissful bachelorhood, brewed himself a cup of steaming hot coffee while simultaneously juggling the cellphone next to his ear. He knew that the coffee would be needed badly – it looked like it was going to be a long night.

Ramesh and Avinash lived in residential quarters located inside the compound which housed the Gurgaon Police Headquarters. So it took them but a few minutes to get back to Avinash's office cabin – which they had vacated only a couple of hours earlier. It was in the office that they got to know the three separate destinations of the vans.

"Call Devesh Malhotra, Rajat and Aradhana," Avinash instructed Ramesh, while still listening to a report coming in on his cellphone. "Wake them up if necessary!"

As the Malhotra family drove to the Gurgaon Police

Headquarters, Avinash woke up his superior and briefed him about the latest development in Bhiwadi.

Commissioner of Police Rajender Saxena was amazed. "Each van went to a factory that manufactures parts used for assembling laser printers? Are you sure?"

"Yes sir! As soon as I got the names I ran a check on Google and also scanned our database of industries. Each of the factories visited by the vans is a small scale unit supplying parts to MCPL for assembling laser printers!"

"Are you planning a raid on these factories?"

"I think, sir, that things have come to a head. The answers to all the mysteries lie in this Centre of Knowledge Complex in Bhiwadi. The final answer, I suspect, will be found in the MCPL factory complex in Gurgaon. The terrorist plot is centered around the laser printers manufactured by MCPL – that much is clear. If we move fast, we may unravel the mystery tonight!"

"What do you plan to do?"

"Raid the Centre of Knowledge and Positive Change in Bhiwadi and the three small scale units that supply laser printer parts to MCPL – all tonight!"

As Avinash spelt out his requirements of manpower and vehicles to his superior, Devesh Malhotra and his daughter Aradhana walked into the office room. They had been asleep when Ramesh Uppal had telephoned.

"Where's Rajat?" asked Ramesh.

"I don't know," replied Devesh Malhotra. "After hearing about the activities in Bhiwadi, Rajat made a few telephone calls and simply took off on his own, in his Pajero, telling Aradhana and me to meet up with you gentlemen here..."

Avinash dropped his phone. "Shit!" he exclaimed. "I think Rajat's planning a raid of his own..."

***

41

The Raid

The white painted walls of the hostel stood out palely in the darkness of the night. The building housed two hundred guest rooms and had four floors. Several dark figures were now sliding up the walls of this building, using a combination of hi-tech wall grips and personal agility. The masked figures were all highly trained commandos of the Special Operations Unit of the Indian Intelligence Service – scrambling up walls like monkeys had been an essential element of their training and they were now quite adept at this.

The seven wall climbers had a specific destination – a brightly lit room on the fourth floor of the building. This room housed a meeting hall – which was now occupied and in use even though the time was well past midnight and the rest of the campus was blanketed in darkness and was deathly quiet.

The first of the masked figures to step on to the balcony that fronted the brightly lit meeting room was Rajat Malhotra. He was swiftly joined by his six SOU colleagues. All were armed with semi-automatic pistols and combat knives, ready for a fight to the finish.

There was now no doubt in Rajat's mind that the Centre of Knowledge was an Al-Qaeda base. Nor was he in any doubt that the two people in the world he most wanted to meet – Rani Suri and Sudesh Aggarwal – were holed up in this campus. All he wanted to ensure was, that these two terrorists would fall into no other hands but his. He needed to know what the terrorists were planning. He also wanted to personally deal with his sister's murderers.

Carefully ensuring that he was not observed, Rajat peered into the brightly lit meeting room through a crack in the curtain.

There were ten people in the room. They were sitting around a conference table, on which was spread out a large-sized map of the world.

Of the ten people, only one was a woman. She was in her mid forties. Dressed in a business-like dark brown trouser-suit, the dark haired woman had a firm no-nonsense look about her. Her thick spectacles made her look slightly older than her years. Rajat had heard Avinash Sharma describe this woman to him not very long ago. He drew a sharp breath – the woman in the room he was staring at was Rani Suri, former Executive Director of Save the Children in Distress Society, the woman who, according to the dying statement of Surinder Mishra, was an Al-Qaeda terrorist.

Rani was pointing at various places on the world map and talking away animatedly.

The nine men in the room looked to be of different nationalities. Three were apparently Indian, while three looked mid-eastern or Arabic and three were of European origin. One of the Indians caught Rajat's eye. He was tall and youngish – about thirty years of age or so – and was very good-looking. The young man's eyes wore a slightly glazed look – as if he was on drugs. Since the other two Indians in the room were middle-aged and portly, it did not take much brilliance on the part of Rajat to conclude that the young man he was looking at, was the absconding Sudesh Aggarwal – his sister's killer.

Rajat pulled out his semi-automatic pistol from inside his jacket and gripped the holster so tightly that his knuckles turned white...

***

42

The Discovery

Eighty policemen were deployed by Detective Superintendent Avinash Sharma for the raids in Bhiwadi. The police contingent was split into four teams. Three teams set off immediately for Bhiwadi to raid the three factories that had been visited by the vans. The industrial township, located on the Haryana-Rajasthan border, was a mere forty minutes drive from Gurgaon at that time of the night – and the police teams were soon waking up frightened night watchmen at the respective factories and getting gates and godowns opened.

Avinash proceeded more leisurely with his team to raid the Centre of Knowledge and Positive Change Complex. His instinct told him that Rajat Malhotra and his SOU colleagues were already on the job. Avinash's immediate priority was to get the Rajasthan police authorities into the loop as soon and as much as possible so that there was no interruption to the Bhiwadi raids. He also arranged for Detective Inspector Ramesh Uppal to lead a police team to the MCPL complex in Gurgaon. He did not know what the police team would find there – but it was now clear that Devesh Malhotra's factory, particularly the laser printer production unit, was central to the terrorist plot, whatever it was.

Devesh and Aradhana agreed to accompany the police team to their factory. The ticklish issue was – which of the MCPL officials could be summoned to help with the searches in the factory complex, without alerting the terrorist plotters? The fact that there was some management connivance was beyond doubt – but its extent was not known.

Avinash and Devesh Malhotra decided to play it safe – they summoned only the Chief Executive and the Production Director to meet up with the police party at the MCPL factory complex.

Eventually, but not very late, Avinash set off with his police team of twenty men to pay a visit to the Centre of Knowledge in Bhiwadi. All the while, information from the other raiding parties already in Bhiwadi kept pouring in over the police wireless and mobile phone instruments.

The vans were still parked in the small scale units raided by the Gurgaon police teams. Their drivers were arrested on the spot – as were the men supervising the unloading of the contents of the vehicles. The vans had been carrying large tins containing white powder.

White powder?

Avinash did not deliberate much on the ethics of his next step. A dreaded terrorist organization was up to some mischief – going by their past practices, thousands of lives could be at stake. Over the phone he ordered his teams in Bhiwadi to put the arrested men through severe interrogation – using third degree methods if necessary.

The arrested men cracked one by one. The information they gave was unsettling. The white powder that had been delivered to the small scale units manufacturing laser printer parts was the powerful explosive PETN.

***

43

Revenge

Detective Superintendent Avinash, who was halfway to Bhiwadi, immediately got in touch with Detective Inspector Ramesh. The latter had reached the MCPL headquarters with his police team and Devesh and Aradhana Malhotra.

"It appears that some of the laser printers manufactured at MCPL are loaded with explosives!"

Ramesh almost dropped his phone. "Are you sure?"

"PETN is supplied to small scale units in Bhiwadi where the explosive is pushed into printer cartridges which are then supplied to MCPL for assembling into laser printers."

"So the Al-Qaeda plot involves bombs disguised as laser printers – now that's a novelty!"

"Not so novel, my friend – they have tried this trick before. Many months ago, the Al-Qaeda sent two such laser printers from

Yemen to USA by different passenger aircrafts. I think they used international courier services. If I remember rightly, a turncoat Al-Qaeda member gave the tip-off, which led to the interception of the bombs before they could do any damage. It was front page news worldwide."

Ramesh felt his heartbeat almost stop. "We must track down these bombs fast!" he exclaimed over the phone.

"You're in the right place to do that – check the MCPL factory godowns for all stocks that may be available and also the dispatch records listing where supplies have been sent. I hope we're not running against time!"

"Are you joining us here?"

"Not yet. I've almost reached the Centre of Knowledge. I suspect Rajat is already here. If he's managed to get his hands on the terrorist leaders holed up here – and if they're still alive – then vital information about the plot could be gathered from them…"

"Best of luck!"

"You'll need all the luck you can get, too…"

As Avinash's convoy reached the gates of the complex in Bhiwadi, Rajat Malhotra made his move.

One of the Europeans inside the meeting room was speaking: "Every problem in this world can be solved, my friends, with the proper application of high explosives – provided you're not around when the explosives go off!"

At that very minute the world exploded around him. Rajat

and his team blasted the windows of the meeting room in a hail of gunfire and stormed in. As the stunned occupants of the room instinctively dropped to the ground to avoid the blitzkrieg of bullets, the SOU commandos quickly took control. Rani Suri and her comrades stood grouped in a corner surrounded by tough commandos pointing semi-automatic pistols at them. Some of the captives cowered with fright, while the others looked belligerently at the attackers.

Rajat stepped forward and stared at the tall good-looking young man with the dazed look. "Are you Sudesh Aggarwal?" he asked harshly.

The young man turned white. He turned and stared at Rani. Rajat had got his answer. He pulled out his combat knife from its sheath. "Come with me," he ordered Rani and Sudesh.

***

44

The Plot

When Avinash Sharma's convoy of police jeeps reached the gates of the Centre of Knowledge, members of the Special Operations Unit of the Indian Intelligence Service met them at the entrance. The SOU commandos had already arrested the guards at the gates and taken charge of the complex. They were part of a larger team that had raided the complex, while Rajat and his six colleagues were capturing the terrorist leaders.

Avinash was led to the front steps of the hostel building. Rajat was coming out of the building. The two men came face-to-face at the entrance.

"Did you find Rani Suri and Sudesh Aggarwal?" asked Avinash.

Rajat gestured upwards with his hand. "They're on the fourth floor."

Avinash carefully studied the face, or whatever he could see of it in the darkness. "Are they alive?"

"Barely."

Avinash drew a deep breath. "Did you have to torture them?" he asked.

Rajat's eyes glittered in the darkness. "My sister died a horrible death – those two devils were directly responsible for her brutal killing. Even my dad and Aradhana were targeted by those monsters with car bombs. There's no need to feel sorry for them…"

Avinash was about to say something when Rajat silenced him with a gesture of his hand. "Many hundreds of people will die horribly if we don't act fast," continued Rajat. "We've made Rani, Sudesh and the other terrorist leaders we captured upstairs, talk. It took some effort – but they've spilled the beans. Their plot is mind blowing."

Avinash's blood froze. "Tell me," he said.

Rajat told him.

As the enormity of the Al-Qaeda plot dawned on Avinash, he quickly dialed Ramesh.

Ramesh took the call in the warehouse of the MCPL factory.

"There are no stocks of laser printers here," he informed Avinash.

"Then we need to know where they have been dispatched!" exclaimed Avinash. "The laser printer bombs that have been assembled at the MCPL factory are supposed to blow up in passenger aircrafts as they fly over South-East Asia, Europe and America!"

***

45

The Packages

An alarm bell rang in Ramesh's mind. "The Director of Production of MCPL, Durgesh Prasad, has gone to the dispatch section to check out documents, to identify where the stocks of laser printers could have been sent!" he exclaimed.

Avinash's brain slipped into fourth gear. "Durgesh Prasad is involved in the plot! Quickly grab him before he destroys key records!"

Ramesh snapped into action. Sure enough, the MCPL Production Director was found in the Dispatch Department, hunched over a shredding machine, frantically feeding dispatch section records into the paper destroyer.

The terrorist conspirator was quickly overpowered. He had been partly successful in his mission – a large pile of shredded paper was recovered from the disposal bin of the shredding machine. Ramesh did not waste time on niceties. Out of sight of Devesh and Aradhana, he and a couple of his police colleagues got to work on Durgesh Prasad. Their interrogation methods worked. The information they needed was soon theirs.

Ramesh was immediately on the phone to Avinash.

From the complex in Bhiwadi where he had stationed himself, Avinash punched his cellphone buttons again and updated Commissioner Rajender Saxena, who was camping in the Crisis Room at Gurgaon Police Headquarters with a team of senior Indian Intelligence officials, with the latest news: "Sir, fifty laser printer bombs have been booked with freight cargo firms UPS and FedEx. These packages are destined to travel in twenty five passenger aircrafts of various international airlines – two bombs per plane!"

The dramatic news galvanized the entire Intelligence community into action. The packages were quickly discovered. The Gurgaon police and SOU joint discovery of the terrorist plot had been just in the nick of time. Forty eight packages were yet to be loaded on to their targeted flights. These packages containing laser printer bombs were lying in the cargo terminal at Mumbai's Chattrapati Shivaji International Airport.

Rajat Malhotra, also camping at the complex with Avinash Sharma, was keeping a close watch on the developments. "Ask them to move the laser printer packages into the double door thick walled vault located in the lower basement of the terminal, until the bomb disposal squads arrive," he advised Avinash. "That way, any explosion, if it happens, will be contained!"

"How do you know about this vault?" asked a surprised Avinash.

"It's my job to know these things," replied Rajat simply, recollecting the staged robbery operation his SOU team and he had conducted at the Chattrapati Shivaji International Airport cargo terminal in Mumbai on the night his sister Anamika had been murdered in Gurgaon.

The terrible reality that now confronted the Indian government – the Prime Minister and the entire Cabinet, the international Intelligence and police community, was that two bombs had already been loaded on to a Qantas Airbus A380 superjumbo that had taken off from Mumbai's International Airport only a few hours before…

***

46

Close Call

Avinash listened carefully to the question that had been put to him over the phone and then looked at Rajat.

"How are the bombs to be detonated?" asked Avinash.

Rajat looked grim. "Let's find out from our terrorist captives," he responded harshly.

The third degree grilling generated results. Avinash relayed the findings to Commissioner Rajender Saxena. "Each aircraft was to carry two bombs. One device was to be detonated through a mobile phone, the other by a timer. The timers are set already – different times for different aircrafts. The bomb disposal squads in Mumbai need to deactivate the timers fast. The detonation of the second bomb by mobile phone was a failsafe option, in case the timer did not work – and was to be done at the time the other bomb was set to go off. Two bombs would create more havoc than one, in any case. There was a lot of careful co-ordination involved – this place in Bhiwadi was the nerve centre from where the mobile phones were to be operated!"

The mobile phones were discovered in a basement room in the administrative block of the Centre of Knowledge. It was the timing of the detonations through these instruments, that was being discussed in the meeting room of the hostel block, before Rajat and his SOU team had captured the terrorist ring leaders. The SIM cards in the twenty five instruments were quickly removed. The cellphones were rendered toothless.

One of the two packages aboard the Qantas Airbus A380 superjumbo was still alive with a bomb primed to explode at the behest of a timer…

The pilots were radioed the terrible news, but it was too late…

REUTERS News Report:

Pilots of a crippled Qantas Airbus A380 superjumbo struggled with more than a dozen system errors late last night and in the early hours of today, after a mysterious explosion occurred in the cargo hold. They landed the plane at Singapore airport with barely any runway to spare.

In fact, the plane was really badly damaged and its a miracle how the five pilots, with a combined 72,000 hours of flying experience, saved the day – and the lives of the five hundred passengers.

A mysterious explosion occurred in the cargo hold of the Sydney bound Qantas Airbus A380, which had taken off from Mumbai's Chattrapati Shivaji International Airport only a few hours earlier, as it flew over Batam Island, Indonesia, causing fragments to rip though parts of the wing, puncturing fuel, hydraulic and electronic systems and leaving the plane with limited flight controls.

The magnitude of the damage became clear only when the co-pilot, acting on a radio alert from India, walked through the cabin towards the cargo hold where a passenger showed him a picture from a camera, mounted on the plane's tail, which fed visuals into the onboard entertainment system.

The picture showed the Airbus leaving behind a trail of fluid – most likely fuel and perhaps hydraulic fluid – from a puncture in the wing.

As the plane lost fuel quickly, its center of gravity also started to shift, presenting another problem. It was not clear how badly the fuel system was damaged.

It took the pilots 50 minutes just to complete the required responses before they could prepare the plane for landing.

The number of errors was so large that computers calculating landing data could not handle them all.

With the plane coming in at 440 tons, about 50 tons heavier than its maximum landing weight, the computer eventually concluded it would stop with just 100 meters of runway to spare at Singapore's Changi Airport.

But 100 meters was enough for the crew and they opted to land instead of dumping fuel, which would further upset the plane's balance.

The A380 "remained barely controllable" (as the captain later reported) as it prepared to land, but it lost many of its systems which controlled pitch, speed and braking, so pilots asked the cabin crew to prepare for an emergency evacuation following an emergency landing.

The Airbus stopped with just 150 meters of concrete left, brakes heated to 900 degrees Celsius and four blown tires.

In addition, it was gushing fuel and one of its engines refused to shut down for over two hours, until fire crews drowned it with foam.

The pilots eventually decided against evacuation and kept passengers on the plane for another hour as fire crews secured the A380.

If the explosion had been of a larger magnitude, the pilots may not have been able to retain control of the plane. A terrible tragedy might have occurred....

***

47

In Memorium

World leaders, led by the President of the United States, personally telephoned the Indian Prime Minister to congratulate him and express their thanks to the Indian Intelligence agencies and police forces for discovering and averting the terrible Al-Qaeda plot which, if it had been successful, would have caused worldwide death and destruction, of unimaginable proportions.

Twenty five passenger aircrafts blowing up in the sky across the world in a twenty four hour period would have not only caused many thousands of innocent deaths, but would have left a trail of shock and horror and repulsion that would have scarred the human psyche perhaps forever. Terrorism had reared a never before imagined spectre of worldwide destruction and death–and nations around the globe geared up to battle this ever growing monster with renewed vigor and greater solidarity.

It was extremely fortunate that the terrorists had been so carried away by the simplicity yet destructive power of their plan that they had plotted a further series of explosions using the same type of disguised bombs–and had sent out van loads of the white powder explosive pentaerythritol tetranitrate (PETN), to the three factories in Bhiwadi, on the night the police surveillance teams had been posted outside the Centre of Knowledge. This had led to the unfolding of events, that had exposed the conspiracy just before the printer bombs could be dispatched to Mumbai airport by regular air freight couriers and loaded on to the targeted aircrafts.

In a small corner of Gurgaon, on the outskirts of the Delhi, a group of people gathered to mourn the death that had led directly to the unraveling of this horrendous plot.

Many thousands of innocent deaths had been prevented because Anamika Malhotra had died young and badly. This perspective did not bring much solace to those who had lived with and loved her.

Avinash Sharma and Ramesh Uppal were back on the lawns of the orphanage with Rajender Saxena not as police officers but as mourners. They had gathered with the Malhotra family and their close friends to participate in a small ceremony, marking the dedication of the small granite stone memorial, in memory of Anamika.

This was also the day that the Save the Children in Distress Society was rechristened the 'Anamika Malhotra Childcare Trust'.

The three orphanages located in Gurgaon, Panipat and Karnal would from now on, be fully funded by the Malhotra family charitable foundations, and would, be closely supervised by a team of nationally renowned social workers.

As the sun set behind the Aravali hills in a golden glow, the little children of the orphanage broke into a song of prayer. Hope was again in the air....

***